ACL

Please return / renew by date shown.
You can renew it at:
norlink.norfolk.gov.uk
or by telephone: 0344 800 8006
Please have your library card & PIN ready

NORFOLK LIBRARY
AND INFORMATION SERVICE

NORFO

30129 0

D1470714

The Dark Entry

OAKMAGIC PUBLICATIONS

Copyright 2009: Debbie & Kelvin Jones

ISBN: 978 1 904330 93 6

First published in 2009

OAKMAGIC PUBLICATIONS
4 South View Cottages,
Lynn Road, West Rudham,
Norfolk PE31 8RN.
www.oakmagicpublications.co.uk
enquiries@oakmagicpublications.co.uk

Printed and bound in Britain

The Dark Entry

PROLOGUE

The teeth of the JCB bit deep into the earth, gouging out a large hole, the arm swinging free and descending again. A screech of metal on metal pierced the air. As the arm juddered, the operator swore loudly, then turned off the ignition. He scowled fiercely, lit a cigarette, then heaved himself out of the cab and peered down into the hole.

"What the hell was that ?"

In the cathedral close, an eerie silence descended like fingers of cold mist, spreading along the length of the close, winding and prodding their way out of the nooks and crannies of the offices and houses, enshrouding pedestrians with a dank odour, like a heavy cold weight in the still, summer air.

The frozen stillness was broken by a low, sustained rumble as if the very earth was groaning and heaving in protest. Like an angry beast, it began slowly, then, gathering speed, began to rock the foundations of the surrounding buildings. From the epicentre, it roared out beyond the Cathedral Close, out to the River, beyond into the city.

At the Ferry, the water began to ripple and churn, rocking the barges and boats, scattering the swans in a macabre flight of fear. A boy, fishing by the river, leapt to his feet in alarm, his stool rocking, his rod dislodged by the deep tremor. Further along the river, behind the magistrate's court, a hunched youth who had been sitting quietly on a bench, sprang to his feet in sudden fear as the trees shook and quivered around him, and the earth moved.

The Dark Entry

The tremor hit the cathedral like a great train, bursting through, rattling windows, shaking joists, scattering hymn books and papers wildly. Terrified choristers gasped in fear and clung to each other as the ancient stones shook to their foundations. Candles guttered and toppled from their sconces and the nave was plunged into stygian gloom as the lights failed.

A party of sixth formers, some lounging on the grass, others cavorting around the labyrinth, fell silent as the tremor hit them and the sky above darkened. Some shrieked, others ran into the cloisters towards the Dark Entry but one girl stood silent at the edge of the grass, sensing the deep reverberations from beneath her.

She clasped her forehead, feeling a sharp, searing pain, then fell backwards in a faint, lying awkwardly on the grass, her ashen face framed by deep red curls.

The JCB operator steadied himself and stared in disbelief. The barriers had collapsed and the JCB was leaning at an acute angle above the hole.
"God help us if there's another of those," he shouted at his workmate. Hands clenched, he stepped carefully over the debris and stood at the mouth of the hole. He certainly wasn't going in there for a while. Crouching at the edge, he peered down and saw part of a lead slab protruding from the clay.

As he stared down, he became aware of a dank, decaying odour emerging from the hole. The nauseating smell clung to him like a piece of musty muslin. He shook himself vigorously, then, lurching backwards, turned and retched.

The Dark Entry

CHAPTER ONE

Luke picked out a double-pronged barb from the box, then reached for the thin nylon thread and began twisting it round the steel shaft encasing the feather.

"Luke ! What are you doing in there ?" called his mother from the kitchen.
"Fishing stuff," came the laconic reply.
"You'd better not be making a mess."
"No, mum."
"Dinner will be ready in fifteen minutes. I want everything cleared up by then. Okay ?"

Luke sighed and returned to his task. He glanced over at the wide screen TV. A man, wearing a cassock, was gazing earnestly at the camera.
"The damage is not as bad as we feared," he was saying.
Luke's fingers tightened on the hook as he laid the fly gently in the box. He thought of his day's fishing and the strange shaking of the earth. He remembered the sharp pang of fear as the world around him had shifted and gyrated. He had never seen the swans and ducks so agitated.
"Fortunately, it will be business as usual tomorrow. Our surveyor will be checking the cathedral in due course."

He gazed curiously at the bespectacled priest. This must be connected with the tremor, he thought. Damn. He wished he'd paid more attention. The reporter was speaking now.

"A number of shops sustained superficial damage. Windows were broken in the city centre. Several trees along the riverbank were toppled and electricity supplies were cut for a period of three hours in the vicinity of the cathedral."

The Dark Entry

Luke peered through the serving hatch into the kitchen.

"Mum. Come quick."

"I'm busy, Luke."

"No, really, it's important."

"Oh, alright. Dinner's nearly ready."

His mother appeared in the doorway. Her long, slim face, framed by short, blond hair, bore an uncanny resemblance to the young man before her.

"Watch !" Luke insisted.

"Mr Jenkins, what exactly happened to you this morning ?"

A broad-shouldered, stocky figure looked apprehensively at the camera. Licking his lips nervously, he began to tell his story.

He'd been operating the JCB in a trench in cathedral close when the digger had hit something. Almost immediately afterwards the tremor had begun. He described the damage that had resulted and how he had feared for his life. He'd been concerned that the digger would topple over onto him.

"Good God, Luke. You told me what happened to you down by the river, but I'd no idea it was so bad."

"Well, you've been in London all day. You wouldn't have known. It was fearsome, I tell you !"

His mother sat next to him in silence. She held him close, then gazed at him.

"You could have been hurt ! I don't know what I'd have done if something had happened to you. Especially after losing your father…"

"I'm Okay. Really !"

Luke pulled away and reached for the remote.

*   *   *

The Dark Entry

At the midsummer solstice Helen and her mother Anne made their way slowly down the cathedral cloisters towards the labyrinth. They spoke softly, occasionally stopping to peer up at the carved figures in the ceiling, intrigued by the ancient faces of characters drawn from biblical history and nature.

"Look, mum ! Look at that amazing green man – so much foliage !" Helen remarked.

"Quite stylised though, aren't they ?" her mother replied. They moved on, necks still craning, peering up into the semi-darkness.

"And look at this one," called Helen. "The face and the leaves are very realistic. The gold leaf looks as fresh as the day it was painted. It's amazing that they've survived."

"Yes," said Anne, "but I prefer yours, more particularly that last green man you painted. He had such strength, he looked as if he had just stepped out of the forest !"

When they reached the labyrinth, they found the quadrangle unusually deserted.

"Oh good," said Helen quietly. "When I was here with the school, it was noisy and I found it difficult to concentrate. When the tremor came, I had the most weird feeling after the pain. I felt that if I'd been standing in the centre, something terrible might have happened. I can't explain it. Almost as if I'd have been swallowed up. That's when I fainted."

"I understand," said her mother. "The energies must have been very powerful."

Helen gazed at her mother. She was lucky to have a parent who was so sensitive and intuitive. Sometimes it was almost as if they knew what each other was going to say.

"Now we'll walk the labyrinth, Helen. You must be the first."

Helen stepped lightly onto the grass. The pattern she followed was familiar to her. She came here often.

Anne gazed at her daughter with affection. Tall and athletic, she stepped purposefully like a dancer around the labyrinth, her long, fiery curls blazing in the sunlight, accentuating her green eyes and pale, smooth skin. She looked like some fey creature from the realm of faerie. She could

The Dark Entry

sense her daughter's excitement. As she reached the centre, Helen stopped suddenly and then, astonishingly, began to spin, slowly at first, then, gathering speed, her arms outstretched, whirling like a dervish. Her multicoloured clothes billowed out as she turned, a riot of reds and yellows, like a great solstice fire. Stopping, she steadied herself and then raised her head and began to sing. Anne felt the power of her daughter's voice as the sound soared up into the summer air. She didn't know her own strength.

*　　　*　　　*

Helen kissed her mother goodbye.

"I'm going down to the water," she said, smiling. "I need to cool down after that !"

"You looked beautiful in the labyrinth, Helen," her mother said proudly. "Like Mab the faery queen. I thought for a moment I'd stepped into the other world."

Helen blushed.

"Anyway, Helen, time's getting on. I'll see you much later. I need to get to the university."

As Helen walked slowly down to the river, she thought of the amazing surge of power she'd felt in the labyrinth. She'd felt a connection straight away. As she had drawn closer to the centre the current had grown stronger and stronger until her whole body throbbed with it. And so her dance had begun and her energy had built to a crescendo. It had never been so strong before. She had staggered slightly on leaving the labyrinth and now felt quite exhausted.

The sun was burning fiercely now as she sought the shade of ancient beech trees at the ferry. A cool breeze met her as she approached the river. She found a quiet space and lay on the grass and closed her eyes and slept.

The Dark Entry

She felt cool and refreshed when she awoke and, reaching inside her shoulder bag, she pulled out a small penny whistle and began to play. Hearing a rustling behind her, she turned to see a tall, blond-haired youth, climbing over the fence. He stared at her.

"Don't wannabe rude," he said, "but d'you think you could give it a rest ?"

"It's a free country, isn't it ?"

"Yeah, but I'm trying to fish."

"It's not as if it's loud!"

"Well, it's disturbing me and the fish!"

He pulled a face and returned to his fishing. Bloody cheek, thought Helen. She stood up, brushed herself down and followed him. She watched him for a while and then approached.

"Am I allowed to speak, or will that scare the fish as well ?"

"Whatever." He shrugged and turned away.

She gazed at the river. How still and peaceful it was, Helen thought. Not a breath of wind in the calm summer air. What a shame he's so rude. *He's spoiling it, not me.* She noticed a pile of broken branches, stacked up against the fence.

"I guess this is the damage from the tremor," she said at last. She never liked to be at odds with people for long. He turned to look at her again.

"Yes. I was down here when it happened. It was weird. I don't want to go through that again."

"And I was in the labyrinth, in the cathedral grounds. School trip. Amazing experience."

There was a pause.

"I'm Helen, by the way," she said, tentatively.

"I'm Luke." There was a pause.

"Sorry if I seemed a bit rude."

"That's OK." Helen smiled. "I'm not surprised you come here to fish. It's so peaceful."

Helen stood up and gazed over the school playing fields in the direction of the cathedral. She could see what looked like a small, dark cloud hanging over the Close. That's odd, she thought. As she watched, the cloud began to move. Slowly at first, then gathering speed, it circled the cathedral. But there's no wind, she reflected. How can that be ? Soon it was moving fast, like an arrow, down towards them, darkening all the while.

"Look at that," she exclaimed. "Luke ! Look !"

Luke stood and turned, his eyes following the direction of her outstretched hand.

"Strange. Is it a swarm of bees ?"

"I don't think so. It's – well – it's a single cloud, but it's as if it's alive."

She stepped closer to him, as a sense of panic began to grip her. The two stood in silence as the cloud reached the ferry and began to descend. It hovered over them, thickening into a dark mass, a twisting, enveloping cloud, blotting out the sun. They both shivered as the cold dank hung, motionless, paralysing them, driving the heat from their bodies.

Then, as rapidly as it had arrived, the cloud moved swiftly off, circling the playing fields, heading back in the direction of the cathedral.

"It's – it's almost as if it was watching us," said Luke in a quiet voice.

The Dark Entry

CHAPTER TWO

From the darkness of the earth it stirred, rising slowly. A dank, cold thing it was, not of this time. Grey and sinuous, it curved this way and that, seeking, always seeking. It rose up above the tall building, then hovered, gazing at the scene below. It noted the small figures moving briskly. Odd shaped carriages moved rapidly along. What strange misshapen world was this ? There was little that was familiar, except for the cathedral buildings. Above the spire, the shape searched for a landmark it could recognise.

Where was the thatched roof of the cathedral ? Where were the woods and the fields ? Where was the canal ? Finally it became aware of the sparkle of water in the near distance. The shape focussed its energy and began to move at speed in the direction of the river, stopping short at the edge of the water, unable to move further, bounded by an old, invisible barrier. Rage simmered briefly, then it turned rapidly, sensing the presence of humankind.

It noted two figures and, drifting closer, began to darken. It reached out to absorb their heat and vitality. It had been too long. It felt hunger and loneliness but its energy was still depleted. It felt despair. Still not strong enough, it withdrew sharply, aware of its feebleness and moved away and back to the cathedral, curling itself around the spire. It rested awhile, then, gathering momentum, it drifted down. Down to the Dark Entry, to that old, familiar place. The sanctuary.

But the way was barred. Some invisible barrier blocked its way.
In desperation, it tried once more. No use.

Frustration engulfed it. It retreated a few yards. Why was this happening ? Memory eluded it.

11

The Dark Entry

At that point the door opened and out tumbled a group of young ones, faces red from singing in the drowsy summer heat, pushing and shoving each other, glad to be released.

The shape hovered as close as it dared, sensing their energy, searching for a suitable host. It would not survive for long in this form. One boy caught its attention. It detected a weakness there, a disconnection, a feebleness that could be fashioned and shaped to its own ends. And so it marked him. It could wait a little longer.

The sound of childish laughter receded as the shape slowly withdrew. Back under the earth, back to the darkness, there to recover its strength.

*   *   *

The pure sound of the boys' voices had echoed through the cathedral, then slowly faded into silence.

"Well done, boys," the choirmaster had said as he'd peered over his spectacles. "Barnaby and Christopher ! You must focus more ! Less day dreaming please. Barnaby, you were at least half a tone out."

Barnaby grimaced, his pale face flushing with embarrassment. He had the look of a dreamer about him, light curly hair framing a wide-eyed, ethereal face. His friends often called him Legolas because of his elfin looks. But he had grown used to it and was partly flattered by the mocking comparison.

The choristers charged at full pelt down the empty cloister towards the Dark Entry and freedom. But they had been brought to a standstill by the strident sound of the choirmaster's voice.

The Dark Entry

"You will walk !" he'd insisted. "Remember who you are and where you are !"

He had watched sternly as they'd walked quietly to the entrance. Once outside, however, they'd relaxed, jostling and teasing each other.

Barnaby had paused in confusion, his attention caught by a sudden movement above him. The air around him seemed to have darkened and he'd felt a deep chill coursing through his body. What was this? Was he ill? His friends seemed fine, laughing and joking as usual. They had continued, unaware of what was happening to him, but he could neither move nor speak. He had been trapped and paralysed. It was as if the life were being drained from him. And then as quickly as it had come, it had vanished.

"Come on, Legolas, what's the matter with you ? We're going to get a burger. We're not waiting !" Christopher shouted. Barnaby pulled himself together, then ran after the others through the car park and into the herb garden.

"Didn't you feel it? The cold?" But by now the others had disappeared around the corner.

As he'd turned the corner, he'd collided at full speed with a tall stranger and recoiled in alarm as the hooded youth swore fiercely at him.

"Watch it !" the youth had shouted. "Just watch where you're going !"
He'd stood there, lean and muscular, feet firmly planted on the path, immoveable, scowling, pushing back his hood, revealing a tense, narrow face, cropped hair and piercing brown eyes.

"I...I'm sorry," Barnaby had blurted, feebly. "I didn't see you."
"You weren't looking where you were going."
"I was miles away. I wasn't thinking."
"You must excuse me I was miles away," the youth had mimicked. "I'm orfully sorry. Mummy's picking me up in her four by four." The boy had begun to enjoy himself.
"Okay." Barnaby flushed. "There's no need for that. Just let me pass, please."

13

The Dark Entry

The boy snorted in disgust, then shoved roughly past him, sending him flying. By the time Barnaby picked himself up and reached the ancient gate, the others had disappeared from view. Deciding to cut his losses, he returned home.

*   *   *

For some while he wandered about the empty house. His parents were still at work and he felt strangely listless and disconnected. He lay on his bed and closed his eyes, remembering the strange feeling he had experienced by the Dark Entry, the sense of panic and paralysis that had overwhelmed him. And the unpleasant encounter with the hooded youth. His thoughts were distracted by the ringing of his mobile.

"Yes, Chris," he said, yawning.
"Where were you ?" Christopher's voice was sharp and demanding.
Barnaby described the incident with the youth. Christopher sympathised and commiserated.
"I thought he was going to punch me," said Barnaby. "It threw me and I felt really tired, so I came home."
He didn't mention the other incident. He didn't know why, but he felt strangely reluctant to talk about it.
"See you tomorrow at school," said Christopher. "Don't forget that book I lent you."
"I won't. See ya."

He needed to chill out after such a weird day. He took his flute out of its case, assembled it and began to play his exercises. The soft, familiar sound of the flute began to relax him. It always did. His music inevitably uplifted him, eased him into a more tranquil state of mind. And so he began to improvise, building note after note into a lilting melody. But gradually the music changed into something more ancient, a slow, intricate piece which normally would have defeated him. His fingers moved along the length of the flute in a dance of their own. He felt both bewildered and enchanted and, as the melody developed, he began to picture in his mind's eye, faint, blurred images of what he thought might be figures moving to a stately dance in some grand hall. It appeared for no more than a few seconds, yet the scene seemed so utterly familiar to him, even though it was indistinct. He *knew* it wasn't just his imagination. He *knew* it was real and it haunted him.

His mother's voice brought him back to earth with a bump.

"Barney," she called, "I'm back ! Was that you playing ? That was amazing !"

Barnaby shook himself, then stood up, flexing his legs. They were stiff and his left foot had gone to sleep. He looked at the clock, astonished to find that somehow he had lost half an hour.

"Hi, mum. Is that the time ?"

His mother came into the room. Her small, rounded presence was comforting and familiar and he gave her a hug.

"What was that piece ?" she asked.

"I don't know," he replied. "It must have been something I heard somewhere," he added feebly.

"I'd love to hear it again." She smiled at him. "But I'm going to make the meal now if you feel like helping."

"I'm just going to have a little rest," said Barnaby softly. "I don't feel very well."

She stroked his arm. "Go and have a lie down," she said sympathetically and left the room.

As Barnaby lay on his bed, he recalled the strange, otherworldly melody and the images it had invoked. How had he managed to play it? Where had it come from and why was it so familiar to him?

CHAPTER THREE

The hooded youth pushed roughly past the boy. He was in a foul mood. He'd had a bad day and that was all he needed, some little rich boy who had it all. A spoilt brat, for sure. He passed through the car park, nursing his prejudice, his face like thunder.

He saw his father, leaning on the digger, smoking a cigarette, desperately drawing the smoke deep into his lungs, looking tense and worried.

"Hi dad !" he said cautiously. His father stared at him blankly for a moment, then pulled himself together.

"Darren ! What are you doing here ? Why aren't you at school ?"

Darren laughed.

"It's gone four."

His father glanced at his watch, clearly confused. "I must be losing it. I could've sworn it was much earlier."

Darren grinned.

His father grunted and looked uneasy. Something was troubling him.

"Something wrong, dad ?" asked Darren, curiously. He was usually so confident and sure of himself. There was a long pause. His father looked away, distracted. There was a look in his eyes his son had never seen before. He seemed almost afraid.

"This your tea break ?" Darren asked, concerned now. His father gazed back at him and then down at the gaping hole beneath them. He realised his dad was still preoccupied with the accident.

"Can't quite get it out of my mind," his father said, eventually. His voice was quiet, his face pale and drawn.

"You mean the accident ?"

16

The Dark Entry

"Yes, Darren, the accident. But I've had a strange feeling ever since. It wasn't just the tremor and the JCB shifting. There was something else. I don't know… I can't explain it. It was after I hit the lead coffin. I didn't know what it was 'til the men came to sort it. There was a peculiar smell as well. It didn't last more than a minute or so, but it made me feel sick, I can tell you."

Darren had never heard his father speak at such length before. He was clearly troubled.

"And I haven't been sleeping well," he continued. "Can't get it out of my head."

They stood, a silent pair, unaware of the toing and froing of passers-by, of visitors to the cathedral, of workers moving through the Close and the raucous cries of a flock of starlings overhead.

"What's happened to the coffin ?" asked Darren, peering down into the hole.

"They turned up yesterday and took it away. Took a while. We wanted to clear up around it but they wouldn't let us anywhere near. Some archaeologist told us it had been there for a long time."

"How long exactly ?"

"About five hundred years. Don't know if there was anything inside it. They wouldn't say. Gives me the creeps. Anyway, now they've finished we've got to finish the job, make up for lost time. I'll be glad when it's over, frankly."

Darren sauntered down to the river, reflecting on what his father had told him. He remembered the day of the tremor. He'd gone to the court with his friend Pete, whose father had pleaded guilty to drink driving. Afterwards he had sat by the river, alone, quietly smoking his roll-up, hoping nobody from his school would see him. When the tremor came, he had felt real fear for the first time in his life. He'd almost expected the earth to swallow him up, as the world had shifted around him. When it had settled, he'd walked round the river path, past the ancient ruined tower, and had stood in silence, watching a young man reel in his fishing line. It had calmed him. He'd gazed around, noting the scattered branches, toppled trees and broken fence of the playing fields.

17

The Dark Entry

"What a mess !" he'd called out to the youth. The young man had turned and grimaced.

"I thought that was it," he'd said, ruefully. "Seen them on the telly but the real thing is something else."

Darren had moved closer.

"Did you see the water ?" he'd asked. "And the ducks went mad."

"Yes," the youth had replied, "and the swans went berserk, too."

They'd looked around, remembering the moment.

"I'm Darren."

"Hi. I'm Luke." He'd smiled at the hooded youth.

"This your hobby then ?"

"I fish a lot, but I like surfing too."

"Where ?"

"Oh I get a lift to the sea at Cromer. Sometimes the surf is really good. Usually when it's rough. You ?"

"Nah. Never tried it. Wouldn't mind having a go at the fishing, though."

Darren had stayed with Luke for a good hour. He'd liked Luke's calm, quiet manner. It had soothed him. He had felt such agitation after the tremor. Luke was a good companion and he was also a good listener. He listened intently to Darren's story about his father's accident and the discovery of the lead coffin. Luke had looked thoughtful.

"Did that happen before the tremor or after ?" he'd asked tentatively.

"Well, he didn't say, but I guess it was before," Darren had replied, puzzled. "Why ?"

"Oh, I don't know. Seems odd, that's all. Odd that the tremor should happen after the accident. That's if it really was after."

Then he'd recounted the episode of the collision with the boy from the cathedral.

"Snotty little sod," Darren had commented.

"Not all the boys from the cathedral are like that you know," Luke had replied. "They're not all rich."

Darren had shrugged in disbelief.

Back in the Close, Darren's father peered down at the empty hole where the coffin had lain. His lack of sleep made him dizzy and slightly

18

The Dark Entry

nauseous. Swaying slightly, he lowered himself to the ground and sat resting, closing his eyes. And so he did not see the thin misty cloud spiral up towards him, out of the earth and up. And as the cloud rose up from the hole, so the surrounding earth began to crack and fracture. It circled him once, then entered. In through the nostrils, winding its way up until it reached his brain. There it curled like a snake and rested. Darren's father coughed, his mouth and nose dry, his head hurting.

*   *   *

Barnaby's mother looked at her watch and frowned. Seven pm already and the potatoes weren't quite cooked. Their guests would be here very soon.

"Barnaby ! Have you finished laying the table ? Has your father appeared yet, or is he still reading in the study ?"

"Yes ! " shouted Barnaby. "I've done the table but he's still in there. And he's not listening to me."

His mother sighed. Her husband never stopped working. Now James was involved with this new discovery at the cathedral he seemed more detached than ever, spending hours at the research institute in his role as a forensic anthropologist. The harsh peal of the doorbell interrupted her thoughts.

"Barney, can you get that please ?"

Barnaby raced to the door and flung it open, revealing the tall, smiling figure of Professor Edwards and his diminutive wife.

"Hello Barnaby. My, you're looking tired. Are you feeling okay ?" boomed the professor.

"Oh yes, I'm fine thanks," replied Barnaby.

He liked Professor Edwards. He had a warmth and vitality about him that struck a chord.

"Come in please," he said politely and ushered them into the lounge. "Mum !" he shouted.

The Dark Entry

His mother appeared, flushed but smiling, fresh from the heat of the kitchen.

"No need to shout, Barnaby," she said severely.

The professor laughed, his face creasing.

"He's fine, Sarah. Just enthusiastic, that's all. Where's James ? Hiding in the study again ?"

James appeared at the door, looking sheepish.

"I'm sorry," he said. "Tim, Frances, glad you could make it."

After the meal, the professor sat back, holding his stomach.

"My my, Sarah ! That was a wonderful roast. Thank you. And so how's your job in the library going ?"

"Oh, very well," Sarah replied. "I'm really enjoying it. And being a part-timer gives me more freedom. And I've been able to do more research about this place."

Frances leaned forward.

"I'd love to hear more, Sarah. The building's medieval, isn't it ?"

"Yes," Sarah replied, enthusiastically. "I've found out from the record office that one of its occupants was a man called Richard Le Prevost. He owned this house in the 1350's. He was a prior at the cathedral. The archive I tracked down described him as a very ambitious and greedy man !"

"Fascinating," said Frances.

"There's still more to find out," continued Sarah. "It's getting more and more interesting as I dig deeper into the history."

"That's intriguing," said Tim. "Sounds like he might have been a troublesome fellow. Talking about digging up information, any more developments with the lead coffin, James ?"

James leaned back and took a swig of wine. His face lit up as he began to describe the discovery.

"Early days yet, though," he said. "Although the coffin was damaged at one end by the digger, most of the find was intact. The remains were in good condition – surprisingly !"

"How old ?" asked Tim.

The Dark Entry

"Fourteenth century, I guess, though we haven't yet done the carbon dating. The body was in pretty good nick. In fact, the clothes, though rotted through, were still just about recognisable."

"A man or a woman's ?" Frances interrupted.

"Oh a man's, certainly. And we're guessing he was of a pretty high status."

"How do you know ?" persisted Frances.

"Because of the quality of his shoes. And we found something else, as well. A leather-bound book, though we haven't opened it yet. There's some evidence to suggest he'd been murdered. Some of his bones, including the spinal column, were fractured."

"Oh dear. That sounds grim," said Frances.

They continued the conversation. Barnaby excused himself from the table and went upstairs to his bedroom. He lay on his bed, wondering about the murdered man and why he had died so violently.

He began to imagine the coffin and its contents. Images came thick and fast now. He saw a wizened skull, white and gleaming in the darkness. It shouldn't look like that, he thought. He'd seen enough of his father's exhibits to know. The apparition stared back at him, eye sockets black and threatening. A strange, dark cloud issued from the mouth, circling the head, almost protectively.

Barnaby recoiled in fear. As the voices in the room below faded, he felt cold, so cold. He was unable to avert his gaze. He stared at the macabre vision and the skull began to change. Flesh thickening around the nose and cheeks, spreading to the temples and the chin. As the face took shape, he found himself looking at a thin, high-cheekboned man of middle years. Heavy, black eyebrows started to form. The face stared back at him, menacingly. He felt nausea spread from the pit of his stomach. It was then he lost consciousness.

CHAPTER FOUR

Darren pulled up his hood, shutting out the world around him. It was lunch time, but cold for a summer's day. As he remembered the tremor he shivered. The shock of the ground shifting beneath him had made him panic. Nearing the cathedral Close, he noticed that the light was less sharp and there was a fine layer of mist clinging to the ancient buildings. He wondered if it was a heat haze but surely it was too chill for that ?

There were groups of men in yellow safety jackets scattered around the area. Curious, he moved closer until he was able to hear snatches of their conversation.

"It's pretty deep," one remarked, pointing towards the Dark Entry.

"There are more cracks than we thought," added another.

They moved back towards one hole, which still lay open and exposed, now shielded from sight by a series of barricades. His father and his mates were working further down the Close. He needed to give his dad the packed lunch he had left at home. He waved and his father paused, then waved back.

He could see more deep cracks radiating out from the hole. One zigzagged down towards the ferry and the river, others spread across the Close towards homes and offices on either side.

"We're going to have to shut off the whole of this area," said an older man in an authoritative voice.

"That's going to cause a lot of bother," said another. "It won't go down well with the cathedral authorities."

"Well, health and safety comes first," replied the first man. "I'm not prepared to take any chances."

Darren moved away and headed towards the group of workmen.

The Dark Entry

"Hi dad," he said, "this looks serious. These cracks to do with the tremor ?"

His father frowned at him.

"What are you doing here ?" he asked, morosely.

"You left your packed lunch on the kitchen table. Thought you might need it."

"Why aren't you at school ? You're skiving again. It's got to stop !"

Darren shrugged and stepped back. He knew how short his father's temper was.

"Okay ! Just trying to do you a favour. Won't bother again !"

His father seized him by the arm and dragged him roughly away from his workmates.

"Don't you talk to me like that ! Not in front of my mates. Next time you'll get a good slap !"

"Okay, okay !" said Darren, shrinking away from his father's red-faced outburst and recalling his anger of the previous night. He was shaken by the suppressed violence his father had displayed. His behaviour had changed recently and it worried him.

"What's going on here ?" he asked, nodding towards the yellow jackets, trying hard to distract his father.

"They're surveyors," his father replied. "They've come to investigate the cracks. They look pretty bad to me. That's all we need. No doubt we'll be laid off."

He stared grimly at the scene before him.

"And now we've got a smell as well."

"What is it ?" asked Darren. "It's faint but it's revolting. Is there a leak ? Is it gas ? Or maybe the sewers ?"

"Don't ask me, Darren. Now then, get off to school. I don't want to see you here again."

Darren left quickly and headed down towards the river. Recently, it had become his sanctuary, a place of retreat where he could collect his thoughts undisturbed. His father's behaviour troubled him deeply. At home he had become aggressive and morose. He'd shouted at both him and his mother. His sister was lucky to be out of it, living in her own flat, with a good job. He felt envious of her. Matters had come to a head in the kitchen last night. His father had lost it. He'd seized his mother by the shoulders, his normally placid face contorted with rage as he shook her again and again. Darren had tried to pull his father away and instead had found himself the focus of his father's rage. He had lunged at him, raising a fist to strike but Darren had caught his arm and had held it like a vice. They had swayed and struggled together, banging into the kitchen table and sending the plates flying.

As they had grappled, his father's face had begun to change and his eyes had widened in surprise at his son's strength. Darren's feet, firmly planted on the floor, grounded him. His father had not been able to move him and slowly Darren had pushed him back against the sink. He hadn't known where his strength had come from but he wasn't going to allow his father to continue. Gradually his father's hold had lessened and Darren had stepped away. His father's face had looked confused and bewildered.

"Dad ?" Darren had asked.

His father had begun to shake as reaction set in. He had held his head in his hands and groaned.

"I don't know what came over me. I just saw red."

His mother had sat down heavily, her face white.

"I'm sorry, Sue," his father had said. "I don't feel right. I haven't felt right since that accident."

"Then you must go to the doctor, Mick," his wife had said firmly.

"I'll see," he'd replied and had lurched away into the other room.

Darren had gazed at his mother, distressed by the incident.

"You okay, mum ? He shouldn't have done that. I won't let him hurt you again."

"Oh Darren. Don't worry. I know he can be bad tempered but he's never been this bad – only recently. We'll get him to see the doctor."

In the sitting room, his father had sat on the sofa, a crumpled figure. His head felt peculiar, unlike a normal headache. A deep pain centred itself above his left eye. It was growing steadily and when the pain reached a pitch, a dark cloud seemed to fill him. And then despair and rage gripped

24

him. It was as if he could hear a voice, deep in the heart of the pain, urging him on.

*   *   *

Barnaby passed through the Dark Entry, tired and irritable. The choir practice had been longer than usual and, once again, the choirmaster had criticised him for his lack of attention. He felt a shiver of apprehension as he emerged into the daylight, remembering his strange experience in this place. On top of all this, his journey home was hindered by the endless stream of cars picking up children from school.

The dank mist was still clinging to the cathedral and, if anything, had worsened through the day. And there was a strange smell emanating from the Close, a rank smell of decay. He wrinkled his nose in disgust.

The large cracks in the ground had been a topic of conversation among the choir boys and the presence of the surveyors had only increased their sense of alarm after the tremor. Flinging his coat and bag onto the sofa, he grabbed a packet of crisps and ate them rapidly.

"Anyone home yet ?" he shouted up the stairs but there was silence.

He entered his father's study. It was peaceful here after all the hassle of the day. The smell of traffic fumes still clung to him and his head ached. He picked out a CD from his father's collection. It was one of his favourites. He settled down in his father's deep armchair, closed his eyes and listened. "The Dark Side Of The Moon" had always fascinated him. He didn't exactly know why. It was so unlike the music of his own generation, but he found it haunting and it allowed him to dream, to escape the everyday trials that often plagued him. The teasing and taunting from the boys at school sometimes drove him mad. The sounds enveloped him totally and he began to drift into a trance. As he did so, it began to change subtly, weaving its spell over him. Images of his choir flashed before him as he recalled the fractiousness of the day. The grotesque faces of the misericords where he sat loomed into view. One in particular filled his vision. It was of an old man, carved in oak, his ornate beard parted in the middle. The eyes held his.

The vision shifted to the high altar, the area lit by a series of tall, flickering candles and he could see the back of a figure, clothed in a cassock. As he watched, the man raised a silver chalice and appeared to bless it. He heard him speak. The sound was not clear but he was sure the man was intoning in Latin.

It was then the man turned and as he did so Barnaby felt a sense of panic. It was the same face he had envisioned before. The same thin, high cheeked head and from beneath those black eyebrows, penetrating blue eyes fixed him with an unrelenting gaze, cold as ice.

The man lowered the chalice to a figure kneeling before him and spoke in a low, sibilant voice. Who was he ? Someone of importance, that was certain. His eyes blurred.

When the vision returned, he seemed to be following him into the Dark Entry. The man paused, then, producing a heavy key, unlocked a door. A door he had never seen before. There were stairs leading to a small, dark chamber, lit only by the flames of a blazing fire.

The man removed his outer clothing, shook himself vigorously as if freeing himself from some onerous duty, then took a black robe from the back of a chair and carefully slipped it on. He moved slowly round the room, lighting candles which had been placed at regular intervals. They formed a perfect circle and at the centre was one black, carved candle, taller than the rest. It was heavy and grotesque and Barnaby caught glimpses of strange reptilian beasts, from another world, their bodies intertwined.

Around the base of the candle stood three small incense burners. These he lit one by one. He raised his arms and began to chant, then turned.

The Dark Entry

Barnaby could see his face clearly in the candlelight. The flickering flames cast shadows on the gaunt, sallow skin and Barnaby thought of the skull and its gleaming white bone. The man reached down and picked up a large, decorated book. Long thin fingers opened it with reverence. Then he turned, holding the book up high, showing it to the boy.

Barnaby could see on the opened page a horned, bearded figure with wild eyes and flared nostrils. The man looked up, staring directly at Barnaby, his dark eyes gleaming. Barnaby cried out, but there was no sound. Surely this was a dream ? If so, he needed to wake now, wake in the comfort of his father's study. But the man smiled at him menacingly, and leaning forward, said in a soft, sinister voice:

"Welcome Barnaby. I've been waiting for you."

CHAPTER FIVE

It was the beginning of the summer holidays and freedom.

"Helen, this is Darren," said Luke.
"Oh, hi Darren."
Helen gazed at him with interest.
"It was your father who discovered the coffin. Luke's told me all about it."

Darren scrutinised her closely. Luke had told him about her experience in the labyrinth. She was an unusual looking girl, he thought. Bit of a new-ager probably. He wasn't sure he could be doing with all that stuff, but he smiled briefly and greeted her. Nevertheless, she was quite a looker.

"Yes, my dad found it. It shook him up."
"How do you mean ?" asked Helen.
"Well, I don't like to talk about my family to strangers, but, since you're a friend of Luke's, I guess it's okay."

He described his father's odd behaviour in some detail.
"It really started after he found the coffin."
Darren looked worried. His face was drawn and he shifted nervously, his body tense and restless.

"Helen and I have been talking a lot about things which have happened since the earth tremor," said Luke. "We often meet up down here by the Ferry. It's too claustrophobic up there by the cathedral. Almost as if someone is watching us."

"Yeah, it's really creepy up there now, especially after the cracks and the smell appeared," replied Darren.

"Do you think it has something to do with the coffin ?" asked Helen, tentatively.

"What d'you mean ?" said Darren.

28

The Dark Entry

"Well, it's a bit of a coincidence, isn't it ? Your dad's machine hit the coffin, then we had the tremor and now we've got cracks and smells and odd behaviour."

"And the mist is still hanging around," added Luke. "And the fish and the ducks haven't been the same since. Still nervous and fearful."

He moved to the edge of the water and gave out a short, high-pitched whistle. As they watched, five ducks appeared, swimming furiously towards him.

"Cool !" exclaimed Darren. "How d'you do that ? Especially since they're so edgy."

"And look, up in the trees," said Helen. "Look !"

Above them, in the branches of the trees, several small birds had gathered. As Luke glanced up, they began to sing, their rich melodies soaring into the air.

"They're singing to you !" laughed Helen. "I've never seen anything like it. You must be a bird whisperer."

Luke shrugged. "It's something I've always done. It's the same sometimes when I'm surfing. Had two dolphins join me the other day. Usually it's only water birds and certain animals. These little finches are a first though."

He whistled quietly back at them.

"My mum says the earth energies have been disturbed by something," said Helen.

Darren snorted in disbelief, but Helen continued. "Well, you can scoff, Darren, but think about a volcano erupting. There must be energy under the earth's crust to create that amount of disturbance and fire."

"Maybe," replied Darren, sounding unconvinced.

"Talking of fire," said Luke, "tell Darren what you can do, Helen."

Helen laughed. "Not a lot really, but I have been doing some street theatre and I've learnt how to do fire eating. Funny, that, because I'm a Leo and that's a fire sign."

She twirled, giggling, her orange skirt flaring out as she spun.

"What sign are you, Luke ?" she asked.

"I'm Cancer," he replied. "July 9th. Maybe that's why I love the water."

"And you, Darren ?" She peered up at his unhappy face.

"I don't believe in all that." His face was shuttered and set.

29

The Dark Entry

"Oh come on Darren," said Luke. "Just for us."

Darren sighed. "Okay, okay. Birthday's on April 29th."

"Ah !" Helen nodded. "Taurus. Strong, stubborn, earthed."

"If you say so," he replied.

"And I'm August 17th," Helen told them. "Not long before my birthday, in fact. I'll be seventeen. Seems I might be the oldest around here."

The two youths nodded. They sat in companionable silence for a short while, listening to the sounds of the river.

"Well, I don't want to go but I'd really like to look at these cracks again," said Luke, resolutely.

"Do you want company ?" asked Darren. "Shall we all go ?"

They made their way slowly up the lane in the direction of the cathedral. When they reached the Lower Close, Luke was alarmed to find that the cracks had increased in number and in depth and the smell seemed stronger than ever.

"I don't believe it," he exclaimed. "It wasn't as bad as this when I was here a couple of days ago."

"It's getting worse," said Darren. He could see his father working away further down the road. "That's my dad," he said nervously. "I don't know what sort of mood he'll be in."

"Don't worry," said Luke as they made their way towards the Dark Entry. "We'll protect you !" He laughed but Darren scowled at him.

"It's not funny !" he said sharply.

As they approached the car park, a slight figure hurtled through the doorway. As they watched, he came to an abrupt halt as if hitting an invisible barrier. His face whitened and his eyes widened with terror.

"What's going on ?" demanded Helen. "What's up with him ?"

"He's the choirboy who ran into me, I'm sure of it." said Darren.

The boy's legs buckled under him and he fell to the ground awkwardly. Helen ran forward and knelt by his side.

"Are you okay ?" she asked. There was no reply. The boy moaned and shook. Darren and Luke crouched by him.

"Looks in a bad way," observed Luke. "Is he having a fit or what ?"

30

The Dark Entry

"I don't know." Helen placed her soft suede bag under the boy's head to protect him from the hard asphalt and spoke reassuringly to him.

The quiet scene was shattered by the loud voice of Darren's father. "What's all this ?" he demanded, his face dark and glowering.

"Oh no," said Darren, uneasily. His father stood staring down at the boy. Helen glanced up, feeling threatened by his presence as his face began to change and darken. His eyes narrowed, focussing intently on the vulnerable, crumpled figure of the boy at his feet. He seems possessed, Helen thought. Maybe that's what's wrong with him. She glanced around but no one seemed to notice what was happening. She felt as if they were in some sort of bubble in time, that they were invisible to the outside world. How could that be? She had always been sensitive to others' feelings and thoughts, had always read their body language and understood their behaviour. Her mother called it her 'sixth sense' but she knew it was more than that. Now she concentrated on the man's face, then, closing her eyes, emptied her mind and opened herself to him. Then the image came. A whirling, grotesque black cloud inside his skull. What was this? She recoiled and withdrew sharply.

The boy began to whimper and she could sense his overwhelming fear of this man's heavy presence. The man stepped closer and the boy's whimpering changed into a high-pitched wail. She couldn't bear it any longer. As the man's lips started to curl in a triumphant smile, Helen sprang to her feet and placed herself between the two figures. She stood, hands on hips, face red with anger, blocking the man's view.

He snarled briefly, preparing to advance but the sight of her strong, athletic figure made him falter. Her clear, green eyes flashed at him, holding his gaze and Darren's father staggered back, clutching his head. He seemed confused, unaware of his surroundings and glanced at the four of them briefly, before lurching off towards the Close.

There was a stunned silence. The boy was sobbing quietly to himself. Helen held him tightly, aware of his fear and of her own fiery strength. It had exhausted her.

"Is he okay ?" asked Luke at last.

The Dark Entry

"That was weird. Sorry, Darren, but it was."

Darren couldn't speak. He felt ashamed and afraid of this strange transformation he had witnessed. He couldn't believe his father could behave in such a way.

Helen spoke quietly.

"You two go on. I'll stay and help him. He needs some peace and quiet. I'll be fine."

Darren gazed down at her.

"I'm sorry that happened," he said, "but what you did, standing up to him like that, well, that was amazing," he said and turned and began to move away.

"See you soon," said Luke. "I'll ring you."

*   *   *

Helen helped Barnaby to his feet.

"Come on," she said, in a kindly way, "we'll go somewhere quiet."

They walked slowly through the Close, towards the river. Barnaby shivered as he caught sight of Darren's father working in the road. He did not appear to notice them, so Helen guided him swiftly past.

Once at the ferry, she sat him down on a bench near the river and gradually he calmed down.

"My name's Helen. What's yours ?" she asked.

"I'm Barnaby Abbott."

"Do you want to talk about it?" she asked. "I'm a good listener."

There was a short silence and then Barnaby spoke in a soft, halting voice.

"I don't know. There have been so many strange things happening. I've just felt so alone. I haven't said anything to anybody about it."

He gazed at her kind face. He didn't know her, but he felt he could trust her completely. In some ways she reminded him of his older sister Kate. He really missed her now she was at university.

The Dark Entry

"First thing I remember was when we left choir practice a few weeks ago. I came out of the Dark Entry with the others and there was something there."

He paused.

"What was it ?" asked Helen.

"I don't know but it was as if something was hanging over me – I couldn't move. It didn't happen to any of the others. I asked them but they just laughed at me. Said I was imagining things."

His voice broke as he remembered the taunts and jibes of the other boys.

"Then what happened ?"

"Then it just went. All of a sudden."

Helen looked out over the still waters of the river. Perhaps he was just an over-imaginative boy, she thought. But there had been strange things happening since the tremor. He continued.

"Things have happened at home, too."

"What exactly ?" Helen waited patiently, recognising his deep anxiety.

"Things have disappeared and I've seen strange things."

"Like what ?"

"I don't want to think about it. It frightens me. Strange shadows. Things like that."

"I see." Helen put her arm around him. "Nothing can happen to you. Don't worry."

"And my dad's been talking about the coffin they found."

"What – the coffin at the cathedral ?"

"Yes. That one. My dad's working on the bones they found in the coffin."

He looked nervous.

"Really ? What a strange coincidence."

"He says the bones are really old. They go back to medieval times. He thinks they belong to a priest, someone very important. And he found a book in the coffin, too."

"What sort of book ?"

"I don't know. I can't even talk about it. I told you."

He remembered the vision. He could see the book clearly, picture the strange drawings. He was sure that it was a book of secrets.

The Dark Entry

"And have all these things happened since the tremor ?" Helen asked.

"Yes. And why did that man treat me like he did ?"

"Darren's father ?"

"If that's who he was, yes. And that's the boy who was unpleasant to me."

"You've seen him before? When you ran into him?"

"That's right."

Barnaby's voice was faint. He looked tired. He needed to go home, she thought.

"I'm going to take you home. Where do you live ?"

"Not far – but I'm fine."

"No you're not," said Helen firmly, "and I've nothing else to do."

Barnaby breathed a sigh of relief. He felt so weary and vulnerable. He was glad of her company. There was something very reassuring about Helen. He felt protected. They walked back up the lane, past the cathedral and out through the gate. It would only take five minutes to reach his house, he had told her. As they moved out into the busy thoroughfare, neither of them noticed the burly figure of Darren's father following them, his face set and grim. He was careful to keep his distance and remain unobserved.

When they came to Barnaby's door, he thanked Helen for her help and disappeared inside. She continued on her way. The man paused outside the house. Raising his head, he sniffed the air, like a hound seeking the scent of the fox, then nodded once and slowly retraced his steps.

Up in his room, lying on his bed, Barnaby recalled Helen's kindness. He had not told her everything. Something had stopped him from telling her about the visions of the past. He felt that if he talked about them, they would become real. That was his secret.

CHAPTER SIX

Barnaby must have slept for an hour, for when he awoke he could hear the sound of voices. His parents must have returned whilst he was sleeping. He stretched and made his way towards the study. In the hallway outside the room he could hear his father's excited voice.

"Yes, the bones are older than we thought. We've carbon dated them. They're from the fourteenth century."

"Goodness!" exclaimed his mother. "So any idea who he was then ?" Her husband leaned forward.

"Well no, but we have found several objects of interest in the coffin."

"Oh, what exactly ?"

"He had a ring on the middle finger of his left hand. Although it was tarnished, we found it was still in reasonable condition. It was embossed with a serpent's head, surrounding a black, jet-like stone. Curious. There was also a black, polished mirror."

"Oh, that's odd," said his wife, thoughtfully. "I'm certain I saw a black mirror of that kind in an exhibition in the museum. As I remember, it was used for scrying, though I can't recall what country it came from."

"That's interesting. Tim thought that's what it might have been used for. He called it an obsidian. But the most interesting thing we found," he continued, "was a book."

"How could a book possibly survive through all those centuries ?"

"It's made of calf skin. The front cover has a series of symbols. We haven't had much time to decipher them yet, but we're going to get John from the university to help us. The strangest thing of all is that none of us can open the damn thing. It looks as good as new, which is very odd, considering its age. And the metal hasp is as shiny as if it were made yesterday. But it won't open."

"How very odd," said his wife, puzzled.

35

The Dark Entry

Beyond the door Barnaby listened with increasing anxiety. He thought of the book in his vision, but it couldn't be the same one, surely ? Or could it ? He peered through the crack in the door just in time to see his father place the book inside a large plastic wallet. His father took the book and then put it carefully in the bottom drawer of his desk.

Barnaby froze. He felt panic well up from the pit of his stomach. The brief glimpse he had obtained was all he needed. He was sure it was the book from his vision, and now it was here, here in the house.

An overwhelming claustrophobia seized him and he ran blindly down the hall, through the kitchen and out. Out into the garden, through the gate and down the alley he fled, his heart racing. He did not stop until he reached the Ferry. The image of the book haunted him and he thought of the horned figure inside. Would it be there if his father was able to open it ? Or was this all in his mind ? Was he losing his grip ? The cruel face of the man in his vision leered back at him. He was a fantasy, nothing more. He must look at the book and satisfy himself or he'd go mad. *I just want to feel normal,* he thought.

*   *   *

Helen slipped her latte slowly. She gazed up at the glass structure of the Millenium Building. It was one of her favourite places. She smiled as she watched the youths outside, some lounging in lazy groups, others skateboarding, a few girls juggling and giggling as the boys eyed them up.

The large, three storey library was a place she had visited often after school, mainly for her coursework. She also regularly searched the Mind Body Spirit section, too, for further information on magic and ritual. Her mother had passed on her wide knowledge of the history of witchcraft and folklore and was teaching Helen a great deal about the use of herbs. It had

36

The Dark Entry

drawn them closer and Helen knew she could go to her mother for help and advice at any time.

She had asked Luke and Darren to meet her here in the busy café where the energy was light and cheerful. She had wanted to share her fears and concerns about Barnaby. When they arrived, she stood up and hugged them both, much to Darren's embarrassment.

"What was so urgent, then, Helen ?" asked Luke. "Not that it isn't nice to see you again."

Helen laughed.

"I should hope so," she replied. She caught Darren's gaze but he flushed and looked away. "I'll come straight to the point," she said. "I'm worried about Barnaby. That's his name. The choirboy."

Darren pulled a face. Helen frowned.

"Let me explain."

She described in detail Barnaby's behaviour outside the Dark Entry. She was careful to avoid mentioning Darren's father.

"I took him down to the river. He was in a real state. Something happened to him in that place but I don't know what it was. He's petrified of going through that entrance."

Darren scoffed. "Duh ! There's nothing there. What a baby. How can he be afraid of a doorway ?"

"Give the boy a break," interrupted Luke. "Carry on, Helen."

"Well, he's convinced that something is lurking there," she continued. "Something dark and threatening. He's had strange things happening at home, too."

"Such as ?" asked Darren.

"He's seen strange shadows, when he's been there alone. And on several occasions he's lost some hours out of his day which he can't explain. He's having weird dreams, too, frightening ones. There's more, but he won't tell me. He's too frightened."

The concern in her voice troubled them, but Darren persisted.

"He's imagining it ! Too sensitive. Give us a break !"

Helen fixed him with a stern gaze.

"Okay, Darren, then here's something else."

37

The Dark Entry

There was a silence. Then she spoke slowly and deliberately. "Barnaby's father is a forensic anthropologist."

"What's that ?" laughed Darren.

She continued, ignoring the interruption. "And his father is involved with the coffin that your father disturbed. And inside the coffin is a dead body. The bones were from medieval times. This is where I think all the strange events have sprung from. The tremor and all those things we've discussed. What a coincidence. And the son of the man who's working on the bones is having a really hard time since the tremor. And I believe him."

There was a silence as they absorbed the information. Then she looked at Darren once more.

"But one of the things that really disturbed him was your father, Darren."

Darren scowled.

"I'm not responsible for him." His voice was hard and resentful.

"I know that," said Helen. "I'm not blaming you. I'm just saying that when I helped Barnaby, I looked up as your father came over and I saw a dark cloud hanging over him." Helen knew she couldn't tell him how much she had really seen. He wouldn't be able to cope with it. Who would, if they were told there was a great darkness inside their father's head?

"What ?" said Darren angrily. "You're making this up !"

"No," said Helen, "I never make things up. I'm telling you what I saw."

"I know Helen sees things sometimes that we don't," said Luke. "We've talked about it down by the river. I believe her. You've said yourself that your father's behaviour is really unpleasant, that he's not been himself. What if something *has* happened to him ? Had you thought of that ?"

Darren stood up, his face tight with anger.

"You're bloody crazy, both of you. I'm not staying to listen to this." And with that he pushed his way through the crowd of customers and was soon lost from sight.

"Darren !" shouted Luke, ignoring the disgruntled looks from the people at the next table.

The Dark Entry

"Oh no," said Helen. "I shouldn't have gone that far but he's so self contained and uptight, I can't stand it." She looked distraught. "And he needs to know."

Luke placed a comforting arm round her shoulder.

"He knows you're right. Just doesn't want to admit it. He'll come round. I'll ring him later."

"Well, I hope so. But I am concerned about Barnaby and I'm going to pop in some time soon to see him. Try to find out more about those bones. But now I'm going up to the library. Thought I'd find out more about the history of the cathedral. Who knows, I may even find out more about who the body is !"

Helen laughed, her natural good humour restored.

"In your dreams," laughed Luke.

*   *   *

Barnaby had become aware of the sky darkening. How long he'd been here by the river he didn't know. He felt a sudden chill as he thought of his return journey home. He no longer considered his house to be a sanctuary. It had been taken over by a malevolent presence that only he was aware of. He began to shiver as he remembered the face in his dreams. The thought of Helen pushed his fear away. He must see her again, soon.

He moved swiftly through the cathedral grounds, heart pounding as he passed the hole where the ever present smell seemed to have thickened and grown stronger. It was a foul, rank stench that turned his stomach. Seeing a movement from the corner of his eye, he whirled round abruptly. In the gloom he was sure he could see a creature scuttling up and out of the hole at speed. God, what was that ? He was visioning again. He ran blindly until he found himself at the end of his street. He paused, panting hard, trying to catch his breath. The street lamps gave a ghostly glow in the vapour trails of mist, a mist which seemed to be spreading. Further down the road, he saw the dark shape of a figure standing motionless, its gaze fixed on one of the houses. Something held him back then, some presentiment of danger, and he slipped silently down the opposite side of the road, taking refuge behind the line of parked cars.

He was close enough now to recognise the figure. It was the man who had accosted him near the Dark Entry. He felt the knot of fear tighten in his stomach like a knife, but soon it was replaced by a feeling of anger and resentment. He no longer felt alone. He could almost feel Helen's presence beside him, urging him on and a surge of strength engulfed him. He was not going to be a victim any more.

As he watched the man raised his left hand and, with fingers outstretched and rigid, made a sudden, sharp, stabbing movement up towards the house. There was power and aggression in the movement and Barnaby shrank back into the shadows. Then he silently retraced his steps back down the road until he came to the alley. The man was now motionless once again.

He slipped quietly through the back door, hoping he hadn't been missed, but he knew his mother would wonder why he hadn't turned up for his evening meal. He hastily raided the fridge, overcome by pangs of hunger. It was then his mother found him. Arms crossed, feet squarely planted, she stood frowning at him.

"And where have you been, young man ?"

"Down by the river. I lost track of time. Sorry."

"And you couldn't be bothered to return for your dinner or call us on your mobile. We were worried about you !"

"I needed some air. Didn't feel too well."

She gazed at his pallid face and her expression softened.

"Well, I must say, you don't look very well. I think it's past your bedtime. We'll talk more in the morning."

Barnaby kissed his mother and went to his room, glad to have avoided a big row. He was very tired and overwrought and needed his sleep. He changed, throwing his clothes in a heap on the floor. He'd clear them up in the morning. He went to the window and pulled back the heavy curtains. He had never been able to sleep with the curtains drawn, he found it stifling and claustrophobic.

He peered down into the street, searching for the man. He must have gone by now, surely ? But no. He was still there. Still staring up in a blank and rigid way, frozen like a statue. *What is it with him ? It's as if he's possessed. Yes, that's it !* Then slowly the man's head moved in a curious, reptilian fashion until his gaze fixed on Barnaby's window. As he peered down the man's face changed and he nodded. Barnaby had seen him do that once before. What did that signify ? And then the man's coarse, broad face broke into a smile of recognition, a cold, sardonic smile. The smile of a hunter who has found his prey.

He walked away.

As Darren's father walked down the street, the grey shadow shifted inside his mind, bending him further to its will. It squatted inside him like a toad, angry and resentful.

I grow weary of this dull creature. He is naught but clay. He vexes me greatly and I long to be rid of him. I will have the boy with his light mind and his weakness that I can meld and shape to my purpose. He is very special. The one. I gave him a taste of my power. The house is mine. And their looking glass carries my mark. They are usurpers, yet the boy will take me in.

I shall enter the cathedral again. I shall.

The Dark Entry

CHAPTER SEVEN

In the Close, the mist slowly rises from the depths of the hole, a dense, cloying mist, full of the dark secrets of the past. Secrets no longer contained. Secrets of dark magic and dire deeds, of lives lost and hopes abandoned. And through the night the mist slowly journeys, carrying the dank smell from beneath the earth, out and beyond the Close. Seeking the crevices and cracks of ancient buildings, it fingers its way forward and outward, always searching, smothering whatever lies in its path. By dawn it permeates the buildings. Children wake, coughing and catching their breath, retching at the putrid stench. It winds and turns along the cathedral cloisters, twisting this way and that, pressing against doors, seeking access. So it spreads out, beyond the river into the city streets where early morning workers splutter and protest at the foul odour.

From the edge of the hole emerges a small, dark shape. It pauses and sniffs the rank air, its natural element. It moves swiftly across the Close, consumed by hunger. Others follow, an endless line of lean, grey bodies, running with intent. More pour out of the hole, as if it were a portal in time, linking past to present.

*   *   *

"Barnaby ! Wake up !"

He stirred. His mother stood staring at him, arms folded, frowning. "I want a word with you." Her voice was strangely hard and flat. Barnaby yawned, then sat up, rubbing his eyes.

42

The Dark Entry

"What's the matter ?" He sensed trouble. "I didn't mean to stay out so long last night, I lost track of time."

"I'm not talking about that," his mother snapped, impatiently. "Get dressed and come downstairs."

She waited by the door whilst he dressed hurriedly, aware of her stern gaze. They walked down the stairs in silence. Barnaby felt uneasy. His mother was normally much more light spirited than this. She rarely took him to task unless it was serious.

"Into the lounge," she said.

Barnaby entered the room and waited.

"Well?" his mother demanded. There was anger in her voice.

"I don't get it !" he replied, puzzled. "What have I done exactly ?"

"The mirror. Look ! Your handiwork ?"

He turned and faced the fire. Above the hearth hung a large, ornate, gold-framed mirror. It had been in the family for three generations and his mother had a great affection for it. The highly polished surface of the glass showed a deep fracture from top to bottom, like the raw edges of a jagged scar.

"What happened ?" he asked, appalled.

"You tell me," his mother snapped. "There are three people in this house and your father and I certainly didn't do this."

There was a silence. His mother clearly thought he was the perpetrator. For an instant Barnaby had an image of Darren's father, standing outside the house the previous night. He remembered the gesture he had made, the sudden jabbing of the hand and he went cold.

"It's quite beyond repair," his mother pointed out.

"But I didn't do this," cried Barnaby. "You can't possibly think it was me ?"

"Who else could it be, then ?"

"But I was out by the river until late, then I went straight to bed. I slept like a log – I only just woke up."

His mother gazed at his white, intense face. There were tears in his eyes and his voice trembled with emotion. For a moment she thought she had glimpsed fear in his eyes. Why was he afraid ? She knew then he must be telling the truth.

"Well…I don't know, I'm sure," she faltered. "How did this happen then ?"

43

The Dark Entry

She sat down heavily on the sofa. Barnaby sat next to her and slipped his arm through hers. How he longed to tell her about the Dark Entry and the visions and most of all, Darren's father. But she wouldn't understand. Suddenly he felt immensely alone and the old fear started to rise again.

"Maybe there was another earth tremor ?" he suggested, quietly.

"I don't think so. Nothing else in the house has been damaged."

His mother patted his arm.

"This will just have to remain a mystery," she said, resignedly.

*   *   *

There was an uncomfortable silence. Barnaby shifted uneasily in his seat. He didn't know why he had come here to Helen's house. That boy Darren always seemed to be staring at him and it wasn't in a friendly way. Why did he dislike him so much ?

"Come on, everyone." Helen sounded exasperated. She had invited them all here to talk and the least they could do was to make an effort to get along with each other.

"I've been looking into the history of the cathedral like I said I would. I've come up with some interesting facts. There have been some weird and unpleasant things happening to the cathedral in the past, as well as the tremor."

Ah, at last I have their attention, she thought, as the youths sat up and responded.

"There was a terrible hurricane in the fourteenth century. It lasted six days. Unbelievable ! The wooden spire crashed through the roof. Then there were the riots and the mob from the city set fire to the place and killed the monks."

"Wow !" said Luke. "And we were worried about a small tremor !"

"Oh, there's more," said Helen. "The cathedral's been ransacked in the Civil War and lightning burned down the spire on at least three occasions.

44

The Dark Entry

Mind you, that's when the spire was made of wood. Once they'd built it from stone, there were fewer fires."

The others looked thoughtful.

"Strange that so many disastrous things should have happened to the cathedral," offered Barnaby, timidly. He expected a sarcastic comment from Darren, but there was none. Darren looked distracted.

"Yes," agreed Helen. "And of course the plague came here too and lots of people died."

"Didn't that come from the rats ?" asked Darren.

"Yes, it was bubonic plague." She paused, watching them closely. "But the weirdest thing of all was this. About a hundred and fifty years ago they were digging a grave near the choir when they came across a stone coffin. Inside was a wooden shell and in it was the body of a man who had died in 1670. He was in almost perfect condition. He must have been well thought of to have been buried inside the cathedral."

She looked up from her notes, wondering how long it would take them to make the connection. It was Darren who spoke first.

"How strange," he said. "And now they've found another coffin. But this one's outside the cathedral."

"Who was he, then ?" asked Barnaby, apprehensively.

"I don't know who he was," said Helen. "But anyone buried inside the cathedral was bound to be important."

"So what if they're buried outside ?" asked Luke.

"I guess they wouldn't have wanted the person inside, so I think we can draw our own conclusions," replied Helen.

"D'you mean he'd have done something wrong ?" asked Darren.

"Maybe they threw him out of the church," suggested Luke, reflectively. "Perhaps he'd done something really bad."

"Yes," said Helen. "Quite likely."

It was then she noticed Barnaby. His face was ashen and he had sunk back down in his chair. His eyes were fixed on the corner of the room and he looked terrified. It was as if he had seen a ghost.

"Barnaby!" she called. He didn't hear her. The others watched him with mounting unease.

The Dark Entry

But all Barnaby was conscious of was the cruel face of his visions, the penetrating eyes, the thin, curled lips. He knew now that the body in the lead coffin was indeed the man of his dreams. He had no proof, of course, nor did he need it, for he knew it was the same person. A man who was utterly ruthless, capable of anything. He was vaguely aware of the others' worried faces looking at him, but they quickly faded from view.

He began to shake uncontrollably. The vision deepened and he gave voice to his fear.

"NO !" he shouted. "Get away !"

He struggled out of his chair and swayed perilously, his eyes wild and staring. But he couldn't fight the power of the man as he was drawn inexorably across the room. His voice became more shrill.

Luke and Darren rose from their seats in alarm as Barnaby struggled to breathe, his face crimson with effort, his eyes bulging. But it was Helen who took control. She knew she must act or he would be lost.

She stepped firmly into his path as he staggered forward, took a deep breath from the depths of her stomach and bellowed:

"OUT ! Begone !"

The fire in her voice cut deep into Barnaby's trance. For a while, his mind whirled in confusion and fear as the vision vanished and he was cut adrift. His legs crumpled beneath him, then slowly he fell.

And it was Darren who caught him.

*   *   *

Helen stood in the middle of the circle. She looked at their shaken faces and realised she had to do something to calm them. Something to protect them all from the dark cloud, the sinister presence which had threatened to engulf Barnaby. She, too, had been shaken to her core, but she knew she must take the initiative and restore a sense of balance. So she had drawn a

The Dark Entry

circle in salt on the carpet, as her mother had shown her, and had created the circle around the perimeter of the room. Luke and Darren sat cross legged on the carpet, either side of Barnaby.

She had called on the four elements and directions, naming them in turn, drawing a protective cloak about the others. She had done this many times before but had never felt such a sense of urgency. She lit the incense burner, then struck the heavy metal singing bowl. The sound shimmered and resonated around them. Darren had looked awkward at first, but now his face had relaxed and his eyes were closed. She began to hum, softly at first, then louder and stronger as the sound of the bowl increased in intensity.

"I draw this circle of protection about us," she began. She glanced at the others. Their faces were calmer now. "May the darkness beyond depart." She began to sing, an old chant of her mother's, a song of strength and safety and courage. Her voice rose and soared with the bowl and the circle seemed somehow to strengthen. Then, subtly, the sound of the bowl began to change. The pure notes began to alter. A discordant, metallic element started to intrude, slowly growing louder. Her voice faltered. What was this, she thought, in alarm ? At last the sound became unbearable. She began to see dark, blurred shapes in the corner of the room. And she became aware of the others' unease as they too sensed an unwelcome presence.

Barnaby's fear had spread through them. She could almost taste it. Now she realised what he had been so afraid of but had been unable to tell her. She felt an overwhelming sense of pity for him.

A dank, fetid smell filled the space around the circle and she coughed violently. From the dark recess of the corner black shapes began to coalesce into one cloud. She could see a face forming, a narrow, pointed face with cold eyes that chilled her to the core. She felt the circle grow weaker and weaker as the saturnine face became ever stronger. She struggled to maintain her grip but was soon lost in the penetrating gaze.

The Dark Entry

Her head whirled with panic. She could hear the protests from the others but they seemed far off now. She must not give in she thought, weakly. But the thought slipped away from her as she slowly sank into darkness.

The Dark Entry

CHAPTER EIGHT

Anne Murray opened the lounge door and recoiled at the scene before her. Her daughter was lying limply in the centre of the room, her face white, her eyes closed. Two youths sat on the carpet in frozen silence, eyes wide and staring. They looked terrified. One smaller boy lay curled in a tight ball between them, moaning quietly. She noted the circle of salt, the smell of incense, and knew immediately what Helen had been trying to do. To her alarm she saw an area of darkness on the opposite side of the room, moving slowly but steadily closer to the youths and pushing against the salt barrier. It spread round the edge of the circle, seeking its prey.

Alarmed now, she could make out wisps of dark vapour entering the circle, beginning to solidify. She could sense its malevolence and knew she must act without delay. She lunged forward into the circle, sending the salt flying in her haste. The dark cloud had almost reached Helen as she stood at the centre and planted her feet firmly either side of her daughter's still body.

She had little time now but she breathed deeply – down into the pit of her stomach. Then she raised her head. She could feel the energy growing within her, an old power, handed down to her through the ages. She took out her bull-roarer and unwound the string. As her power found its voice, so she began to whirl it around her head with increasing speed, until all that could be heard was an explosion of rage and the loud humming song of the bull-roarer.

She could feel the heat within her. Every fibre of her being resonated as her magical energy reached a crescendo. She was caught up in the vortex of power she had summoned and she knew she must control her anger and strength and focus it into a weapon, a form of words that would pierce the shadow and scatter it. Ancient words they were, words she had acquired

over years of study into the history of magical ritual. And once uttered, the
words shimmered, then coalesced into the shape of a spear and the spear
flew straight and true and pierced the centre of the black core of the cloud.

She heard a shrill cry of pain and rage as the black cloud retreated, then
dispersed to the corner of the room. Still she pushed it further and drove it
from the place.

Anne stood at the centre of the circle and shook, shook with utter
exhaustion. It had taken her all her strength to fight this thing that had
entered her house and threatened her daughter. She slumped to her knees
and shivered as the strength drained from her. She felt deathly cold as
reaction set in.

Pale faced, Luke struggled to his knees, dazed and frightened by what
had happened. He crawled over to Helen's mother. Who else could it be,
he thought ? He touched her shoulder gently and she turned to him, her
face drawn.

"Are you okay ?" he asked, faintly. She sounded winded as if she had
been punched in the stomach and was unable to find her voice.
"They okay ?" she whispered, nodding towards the others.
"I'll see," he replied, and standing up, made his way over to them.
Darren was sitting upright now. He looked shocked and bewildered, but he
grinned weakly back at Luke. Barnaby was silent but alert, staring
anxiously at Helen.

Luke carefully placed a cushion under Helen's head. She was deathly
cold, her face was ashen and her breathing shallow. He pulled a patchwork
blanket from the sofa and wrapped it round her chill form.

*   *   *

The Dark Entry

The animate cloud spiralled and twisted away from the house. Over the roofs it soared in rage and pain, seeking out its host. The spirit within the cloud had gathered enough strength to enter and leave its host as it so desired but it was not yet strong enough to withstand such an attack.

It raged its way through the streets, invisible to passers-by, but gradually it weakened. It needed its host urgently. His strength and life-force were essential, or it would sputter, then fade like the last flame-burst of a dying candle.

The spirit found Darren's father as he sat eating a sandwich with a workmate. It slid silently into its victim and curled like a serpent inside his mind.

*   *   *

Anne Murray pushed open the door to the lounge and entered, bearing a large tea tray.

"You had me really worried," she began, as they drank their tea in silence. "I don't know what came over you. Helen," she said stiffly. "You know you should never play games with the unknown. After all I've taught you, you still have a lot more to learn."

Helen flushed with embarrassment, recalling the events of the afternoon. She'd never known such fear before.

"I need to explain, mum," she said quietly.

"You certainly do, young lady," her mother replied. "I want to understand why you did it."

There was an awkward silence. All four of them were still shaky from the effects of what had happened. It was then Barnaby spoke up in his small, quiet voice. He told Anne everything. About the weird goings on in his house, about his father's work with the coffin and the bones and the discovery of the ancient book.

The Dark Entry

"But there's more, Barnaby, isn't there ? I can tell." Anne smiled reassuringly at him, sensing a deep and hidden fear. "You can trust me. I know something of these things."

When Barnaby went on to tell her of the visions and of the man with the cruel face, she looked perturbed.

"I don't think it was modern day," Barnaby continued. "He was wearing really old-fashioned robes – not like the priests wear these days, and there was no electricity – just loads of candles. It was smoky and dirty."

Anne looked thoughtful.

"What did he do ?" she asked intently.

"He went to a room – I think it was above the Dark Entry. Did there used to be a room there long ago ?" he asked.

"I can find out," she said, reassuringly.

"Well he went up into the room. It was dark except for the light of a big fire. The flickering flames made it look really spooky." He paused, remembering. "He put on a black robe and lit a circle of candles. They were big and the one in the centre was black."

Anne nodded, knowingly. "I see. Go on," she said, her voice grave and subdued. The others looked uneasy and were shifting nervously in their seats.

"There seemed to be a lot of incense burning – it was very smoky in there – and then he picked up a large book." Barnaby stopped abruptly sensing the old fear returning.

"Yes. Carry on," said Helen. She was intrigued now.

"I could see him open the book and I saw the first page. It was a picture of…" He paused. "… of a figure with horns and wild hair and the eyes…"

"Yes, what were the eyes like ?" asked Anne, insistently.

"They were…red and staring."

"And then ?"

"And then the vision disappeared, but before it did, the man turned. He seemed to look straight at me, and then he said something."

There was an expectant silence.

"He said: "'Welcome Barnaby.'" Barnaby's voice faltered and he put his head in his hands.

The Dark Entry

Darren watched Barnaby carefully. He hadn't realised Barnaby had been subjected to all this. Suddenly he felt immensely sorry for him.

"And is there more, Barnaby ?" asked Anne in a kindly voice. Barnaby looked up, glancing nervously at Darren.

"Well, I don't like to say..." he stammered.

Darren spoke. "It's about my dad, isn't it ?"

Barnaby nodded, his face red.

"Yes, it is. I'm truly sorry, Darren, but it is."

"Well it's okay. Tell us."

Encouraged, Barnaby continued. He told them of the strange behaviour of Darren's father towards him and that when he'd seen him near the Dark Entry, he'd looked as if he were possessed. Darren bit his lip with apprehension. It was when Barnaby told them of Darren's father's appearance outside his house and his constant upwards gaze at Barnaby's room that Darren began to realise the extent to which his father had changed. Barnaby described the strange gesture and the subsequent cracking of the mirror, found the next day. Darren groaned.

"I knew there was something wrong with him at home but I hadn't realised he'd got so bad."

Barnaby was overwhelmed by a sense of relief.

"I haven't told anyone else about the visions," he said. "I've told Helen some of the rest but not about those. It's been awful. I've felt so alone."

Helen hugged him. "It's okay, Barnaby. You're safe with us. If anything else happens we'll be straight round to your house, don't worry."

Barnaby smiled and for the first time Helen saw him fully relax.

"That's better," she laughed. "Let's have some cake."

They chatted quietly through more tea and cakes. The mood in the room had lightened considerably but they were greatly affected by the experience.

"Hey," said Luke, grinning. "I'll take you surfing, Barnaby. That'll take your mind off things."

"I'd like that, thanks."

Anne returned from the kitchen.

53

The Dark Entry

"I have something to give you all," she said, seriously. She reached into her apron pocket and pulled out a small, velvet bag.

"I have these for you," she said as she took out four stone pendants and laid them carefully on the carpet.

"What are they?" asked Luke, leaning over to examine them closely.

"They're rune stones, but also runes of protection. Normally I'd carve them out of wood but there's no time."

They sensed an urgency in her voice as she continued. "Helen told me your birth dates earlier. I hope she got them right. It's interesting that each of your birth signs represents the four elements."

"Earth, air, fire and water," added Helen.

"Yes indeed," replied her mother. "Helen is fire of course. Sometimes I think she has too much fire in her." She smiled fondly. "So this is your protective rune, Helen."

She placed the small, white quartz stone pendant in front of Helen and on the flat surface of the stone she had painted a symbol.

"This represents fire, Fehu, and earth. Earth to keep you grounded, fire to give you strength."

Then she turned to Luke.

"And this is for you – you're a young man of the water, I gather, water and wildlife – a good combination."

Luke looked at the rune. It had the same base as Helen's but the top was different.

"This is the water sign, Laguz," Anne said, "and you have the grounding rune as well. Water may well prove to be your protection," she added enigmatically and smiled. Luke thanked her.

"And you, young man, well I can feel your strength from here."

Darren grinned shyly. No one had praised him in such a way before.

"Yours is a double earth sign, for earth is your strength. It is Elhaz."

Darren took the stone pendant and gazed at it. He wasn't used to all this stuff but when he held the pendant tightly, he thought he felt a shiver run up his arm. Maybe he'd imagined it, but after what he'd seen and heard this afternoon he was willing to try anything. Finally Anne turned to Barnaby.

"And you, Barnaby. You have the power of air, I believe. Your music and your voice are your strengths. You too have the grounding rune at the base. You need to be earthed more, feel stronger – and you have the rune of the breath, the voice, Ansuz."

Barnaby took his rune stone and gazed at the symbol. It reminded him of some of the musical notes in his song sheets. How odd, he thought, that the rune should reflect the notation in his musical scores. He grasped the pendant and he too felt an immediate sense of warmth from it.

"Thank you," he said, smiling at Anne.

"Just one last thing," said Anne. "Whatever lies ahead, be sure to keep the amulets with you. They will be of great service to you. Each stone only reflects the element of your birth. The stone will help you tap into your energy. But remember: that energy is within you !"

She watched as all four slipped the leather strings over their heads. Each one touched the stones tentatively and then fell silent for a while.

CHAPTER NINE

Darren and Barnaby walked slowly along the road. They had much to think about. Barnaby recalled his vision with fear but had been comforted by his runic gift and Anne's strong supportive presence.

Darren was confused and afraid when he thought of what had happened to his father. He could hardly believe the events that had taken place in Helen's lounge and yet he had seen it with his own eyes. Admittedly he hadn't glimpsed the face of the vision, just the black cloud. But he'd been totally convinced that both Helen and Barnaby's fears were very real. He glanced down at Barnaby. He felt sorry for the boy, sorry that he'd been so unpleasant to him. Ashamed that he'd scoffed and sneered and hadn't believed him. And now they were making their way back to the cathedral towards the Dark Entry.

"There's nothing to worry about," said Darren. "I'll be with you."

"But I can't do it," replied Barnaby in an anxious voice.

"I won't let anything hurt you," said Darren, firmly. Barnaby was so vulnerable and so weary, thought Darren. If he doesn't do it now, he never will.

"I've tried several times through the holiday to go through that door, but each time I've done it, I've panicked so much I've had to go the long way round."

"Look," said Darren, after a pause, "I know you are afraid, but if you can, just bring yourself to do it once, then the next time will be a lot easier. It's like falling off your bike, you have to get straight back on again or you'll lose your nerve."

"I know," replied Barnaby. "Maybe I can do it with you there. You know all about it but the others all laugh at me. They think I'm a joke but they haven't seen what I've seen."

"Well," said Darren firmly, "let's give it a go, shall we ? Yeah ?"

The Dark Entry

Barnaby nodded but he still looked apprehensive.

They crossed the by-pass and made their way through the busy streets until they reached the Ethelbert Gate. They gazed up at the figure of St George fighting the dragon.

"There you are !" laughed Darren. "That's you. Think about it."

Barnaby smiled shyly at him. He was glad he was with Darren. He had such a feeling of strength about him. He might be a little rough and down to earth but he was strong and knew how to handle himself.

They passed through the gate and made their way down to the herbarium garden. The smell of lavender and rosemary was almost overpowering as they passed through and into the car park next to the refectory. Barnaby paused briefly, and then, as if mustering his strength, strode purposefully towards The Dark Entry.

Unusually, the car park was almost empty and he was glad that there were few people about. He didn't want an audience. It was almost the end of the long summer holiday and he HAD to do this before the new term started.

As they drew close to the very place that Barnaby feared, the quiet stillness of late afternoon was ruptured by the sound of an angry bellow. Darren and Barnaby spun round. There, staggering towards them in a strangely disjointed, lurching manner, was Darren's father, face red with effort, eyes bulging, but oddly blank faced. His hands reached out to them like two immense claws.

"That isn't my father," said Darren in a cold voice. "It's that thing inside him. Run, Barnaby, run !"

And Barnaby ran with terror snapping at his heels, Darren's father staggering after him with Darren close behind. It was like a scene from an old silent movie, Darren thought. What was it *? Frankenstein. That's what his father looked like, his face distorted and twisted. A thing possessed.*

He sped around the side of the cathedral, alongside the south door, past the lady chapel, until he had to stop for breath. It was a quiet spot, a grassy, secluded area with no one around and it was here that the man finally caught up with him.

Barnaby shrank back against the stone wall of the cathedral. The man was close now, reaching for him feverishly. It was then he saw Darren slide swiftly between him and his father.

"Dad ! Wake up !" shouted Darren, but his father's face did not change. Darren stood like a wall of stone, facing his father, who shoved roughly against him. His hand moved instinctively to the runic amulet at his chest. He concentrated hard and felt a surge of raw power rise up through his legs and torso.

He took a step forward and held his father by the shoulders, his feet rooted to the ground like a giant oak, unshakeable, immoveable. But his father was also strong. He reached for Darren's throat and began to grip hard. They struggled like great wrestlers, swaying back and forth, unable to move each other.

"Must ... touch... the ...boy !" his father growled in a voice Darren could not recognise. It was a deep throated, almost metallic voice. Darren's strength wavered briefly. This was not his father, yet he could not hurt his father's body.

As they stood braced against each other, he saw his father's blank eyes begin to focus. First they stared at the cowering Barnaby behind Darren, then the head shifted slightly until Darren found himself the object of attention. He saw the eyes begin to change, the pupils becoming sharp pinpoints of concentrated fury and frustration.

"I *will* have him !" The voice from his father's mouth was low and menacing and the eyes bored deeper into his soul, holding his gaze. Darren struggled to move his head but he could not. His strength was beginning to fade and he felt instant, paralysing fear. Would this thing, this creature, take him too? It was when he began to lose his grip that the struggle was cut short by a loud, clear voice.

"What's going on here? What exactly are you doing?"

58

The Dark Entry

His father's head turned to seek out the intruder who had so rudely interrupted him. Darren, released from the hypnotic gaze, struggled to free himself. He saw a man approaching dressed in a cassock, annoyed that anyone should dare to fight in this hallowed space.

The spirit inside Darren's father twisted the heavy, ungainly body around to face this new entity. It noted the sharp, intelligent face, a face not unlike that of his old self, the black cassock denoting his status within the cathedral. Ah, how it longed to be in there once more. The boy could wait. There would be another time for him. But now – this was an opportunity not to be missed. How he longed to be rid of this dull, lumpy body.

The verger stepped forward and grabbed hold of Darren's father. That was his mistake. He gazed up into the dark, thunderous face and as he did so, his gaze was caught and trapped like a fly in amber. It was then the mist descended.

Darren stared in amazement as he retreated. He watched in horror as a trail of vapour issued forth from his father's mouth, engulfing the head of the verger. His father reeled backwards, arms flailing to keep his balance, then he fell to his knees, grasping his head.

Darren looked back at the verger, remembering the dark cloud in Helen's room and finally he understood the significance of what had taken place. The verger staggered momentarily, face pale, eyes closed, and then, suddenly, he straightened himself and turned to face Darren and Barnaby.

Barnaby had cowered against the stone wall and had watched the struggle with growing despair. He knew the verger and he too realised what this spirit had done. The verger looked at him and smiled. One cold, triumphant smile. A smile to dash hopes and render despair. He spoke one word to Barnaby:

"Later," he said.

Barnaby fled.

The Dark Entry

CHAPTER TEN

In the long, hot, final week of the summer holidays that followed, the four friends met up as often as they could. Sometimes for coffee and a film, sometimes for a walk by the river. Helen showed them a little of her fire eating. Luke introduced Darren to the art of fishing while Helen and Barnaby played music together. On Helen's birthday, they'd caught a bus to Cromer. It was a hot day and they ate fish and chips and lolled on the sands. The bonds of friendship were strengthened and Barnaby felt comfortable and safe. Luke told them of his father and of his death in a car crash. They had been travelling on the M1 late at night when his father had fallen asleep at the wheel. The car had gone into a concrete pillar and his father had been killed instantly but Barnaby and his mother had survived with only superficial injuries. He explained he had been only seven at the time but his mother had never really got over it. She relied too much on him. The others were sympathetic to him.

Slowly things began to change. Perhaps it was the heat or perhaps it was something much darker that caused people's behaviour to alter.

It began in a small way. Groups of students would gather in the area of the Close and down by the river where they would drink and taunt passers-by. Walkers began to avoid the area, alarmed by their aggressive behaviour and language. Gradually others started to arrive, whether attracted by the darkness of the place or by the over sensational reports in the local papers of the increasing drunkenness and bad behaviour. Perhaps it was both, but the area around the cathedral seemed to draw them like a magnet.

Inevitably, fights developed and gangs rampaged around the surrounding streets, often hurling missiles at passing cars. It came to a head on the Friday night when a student was stabbed at the Ferry. The

60

The Dark Entry

police were called and several youths from out of town were arrested. There was an enormous increase in the incidence of road rage, of street muggings and the gradual acceleration of the levels of aggression in everyday life.

Luke also had been attacked whilst fishing near the ferry. A large, flabby, red-faced youth had appeared suddenly, smelling of drink. He had kicked Luke's fishing tackle bag viciously and then lurched towards Luke himself. He tried to push Luke into the river, laughing all the while. Although Luke was not violent by nature, resentment at the despoiling of his sanctuary by this yob and many others in the last week surged through him. He'd raised his fist and smashed it into the yob's face.

A feeling of pleasure surged through him as he watched the youth struggle and fall, bleeding from the nose. But the pleasure soon turned to disgust and he felt tainted by what he'd done. He'd been aware of the growing violence in the area and he felt contaminated by it. He knew he must fight that or be overwhelmed by it as were so many others. He was beginning to understand where all this dark energy was coming from.

*　　　*　　　*

"Oh, you must be Helen. Come in, dear."

Barnaby's mother smiled at the young, flame-haired woman at the door. "I've heard so much about you. Barnaby talks about you all the time. I'm Sarah, by the way."

Helen smiled and entered.

"Thank you," she said. What a fascinating house. It must be very old."

"Yes it is. Very old. Medieval, in fact. Actually, I'm glad you could come for tea, Helen. Barnaby's been looking forward to it and he's a little depressed about returning to school tomorrow."

"I know," replied Helen, frowning slightly. "I'm not too keen either."

The Dark Entry

"I've more information about the house as well which I hope you'll find interesting," added Sarah.

"Oh yes, I am very interested. Barnaby has told me a little about the man who originally lived here."

They sat in the kitchen, enjoying the afternoon sunlight. It filled the room with a golden hue, bringing warmth and comfort to them. Barnaby chattered brightly as his mother poured the tea.

"I don't know how many people bother to sit down to a traditional tea any more," said Sarah with a smile. "I hope you weren't expecting pizza or chips?"

Helen laughed. "Oh no," she replied. "This is a real treat." She gazed at the mouth - watering cakes that filled the table. Cream buns, carrot cake and lemon drizzle.

"Do help yourself, dear," said Sarah.

There was a comfortable silence save for the sounds of eating, interspersed with the occasional "mmm."

"Well, Barnaby," said Sarah. "I've found out some more information about our house and the reprobate who lived here in the fourteenth century. You may remember."

Barnaby fancied the room had darkened slightly as his mother spoke.

"Oh, right," he replied. "What, exactly?"

"Well, to put it mildly, he was a bit of a naughty boy."

"Ooh." remarked Helen. "That sounds interesting."

"Well yes. Let me just get my notes." Sarah fetched her notebook from the kitchen drawer. "Now let me see. Ah, here we are. He was brought before something called the Star Chamber."

"What was that?" asked Barnaby.

"It was a kind of church court used for serious offences. It's all here in the records. He was accused of two things. The first offence was quite shocking for those days. Apparently, he had a housekeeper who became pregnant. She claimed he was the father and that they had been having a relationship for some while. A number of witnesses came forward to testify against him."

"But why was that so serious?" asked Helen.

The Dark Entry

"Oh, it *was* serious in those days, Helen. Very serious, especially if you were a priest. Priests in those days weren't allowed to marry. They had to be celibate. But there was something else as well."

Barnaby and Helen glanced at each other, intrigued. Barnaby began to feel uneasy.

"The other, more serious offence was to do with his conjuring of spirits."

Barnaby shrank back in his chair. Helen could feel the tension in him.

"Apparently, he had been conducting rituals in order to gain power for himself. The court accused him of being a necromancer, of raising the dead, of dabbling in the black arts."

There was a silence in the kitchen as all three absorbed the information. Sarah finally broke the silence.

"Hope all this doesn't alarm you?" she said. "It was a very long time ago."

"Where would he have done his rituals?" asked Helen.

"Hopefully not in the kitchen, Helen," laughed Sarah, attempting to lighten the mood. "No. Just joking. No need to worry. Apparently it took place in a room somewhere in the cathedral, which is why it was such a sacrilege. I have more photocopied material I need to sort through but that's it for now," she concluded. "Anyway, I'm sorry but I have to leave you now, Helen. I have a meeting at the library and I'm afraid I can't miss it."

"Oh, that's a shame. But thanks anyway for the lovely tea."

"You're welcome," said Sarah as she got up to leave.

"You're not leaving as well, are you, Helen?" asked Barnaby. He had such a forlorn look on his face that Helen laughed.

"Of course I'm not! I came here to spend time with you."

"Oh thanks." Barnaby looked relieved.

"I've a lot to tell you, Helen," he said, "and it's not that pleasant."

He told Helen about Darren helping him at the Dark Entry and of his father's attack on both himself and Darren. Helen was appalled. It was when he told her about the verger that she began to look distinctly afraid.

"So you're saying this… thing has been inside Darren's father and now it's moved into the verger?"

The Dark Entry

Her voice rose with concern. "This is very serious, Barnaby. You had a narrow escape. So did Darren. How's his father ?"

"I'm afraid I ran away but I did ring Darren and his dad's okay. He doesn't remember anything about it."

"Thank goodness for that," said Helen. "Poor man. And now that creature will be in the cathedral. Don't you see, Barnaby ? Don't you see the connection between the man who lived here and this "spirit" ? That's what it's been after all along. To gain access to the cathedral. It has to be the same man that they found in the coffin in the Close. Don't you think ?"

"I knew from that time in your house. I knew it had to be him," replied Barnaby. "What does he want now ? What's he going to do next ?"

*   *   *

It took a while for Barnaby to calm down but eventually he took Helen into the study. The late afternoon sun warmed the room. The rosewood coffee table gleamed in the soft shards of light. Helen immediately crossed the room and gazed up at the vast collection of books that Barnaby's parents had acquired. Her fingers lightly touched the embossed spines of leather and the tooled, suede-bound volumes, as she admired their craftsmanship.

"I love the feel of old books," she sighed. "There's so much history here. Imagine, all those writers. What tales they have told. And this is a wonderfully calm room," she added, turning to smile at Barnaby.

"Yes. I often come in here when my parents are out. Sometimes I play my flute in here. But I haven't done it since I…"

"Since what ?" asked Helen.

"Oh, never mind," said Barnaby, briskly. "I want to show you that book I told you about. My father still has it here. I don't know if he's supposed to keep it. I've only glanced at it, but I wanted you to be here, to help me. It's that face in my vision – you know – the one that looks like a wild man."

The Dark Entry

"With red eyes – yes, I remember. Don't worry. We'll look at it together."

"It's here. In this bottom drawer."

Barnaby pulled out the large drawer. "Do you think you could get it out for me ?"

Helen found herself gazing down at a large plastic wallet. She opened the wallet very carefully and pulled out the book. It was very old with black, scored covers, but remarkably well preserved.

"But it's quite amazing," she said, softly. "Exactly how old is this book ?"

"I heard my dad talking about it to his friends from the Uni. It dates from the fourteenth century, he said. He called it a – what was it ? – a grimoire, I think."

"Ah. My mum knows about these. She'd be interested in seeing this book. She told me a grimoire was a book of spells."

Barnaby fell silent. He knew it already. He knew what he would find inside if only they could open it.

Carefully, Helen placed the book on the desk top. It was bound in red leather which had faded very little considering its immense age. It carried a musty smell of ages long past and she wondered what unpleasantness might lie within its pages. She shivered.

"But they can't open it. It's locked with this brass hasp. They all tried but they didn't want to damage the book." Barnaby watched Helen anxiously. "Do you think you might have a go ?"

"I'll try," said Helen. She took a deep breath, stroked the leather once, seized the hasp, then pushed with her forefinger. Nothing happened. She tried again, with more force this time, but still no luck.

"I don't want to damage it, Barnaby," she said. "You have a go."

"I don't know if I can."

"Go on," she urged. "Try !"

Barnaby felt a strange spark as he touched the leather cover. He pushed at the hasp and immediately it clicked open as if it had been waiting for his touch.

"Wow !" gasped Helen. "Clever you. Now open it."

The Dark Entry

With some trepidation Barnaby opened the book. There, on the title page in black gothic script was an inscription which read: LIBER NECROMONICON. Barnaby fingered the thick vellum pages. "It's not like paper," he said. He turned the stiff page and then recoiled, for in front of him was the creature of his vision.

"I knew it," was all he said.

Helen gazed at the figure who returned her look with a wild, primitive stare. The red eyes gleamed back at her with a fierce intensity she found unnerving.

"Oh, poor you," she said, turning to Barnaby. "Now I understand how you must have felt."

Barnaby turned the page again. The gothic script continued, but this time it was illustrated by small demonic faces that peered and leered grotesquely back at them from all angles of the page. Helen looked closely at the lettering.

"This is Latin," she said. "I've seen it before. My mother might know what it means. There's Latin in the cathedral, too. You must see it all the time. Don't you have to sing in Latin ? I'll try to read it out." She cleared her throat and began to read aloud.

"*Conjuro vos demones in hoc circulo sculptos* – oh, I think I can guess that. It must be to conjure those demons - and look ! *Sculptos*. That must mean something like sculptures or carvings. And it mentions a circle – *per virtutem et potentiam majestatis divine*. That must mean divine majesty. Then there's a bit I can't read properly and now there seems to be a list of names."

She fell silent as she read the strange, alien names until she came to one she recognised.

"I think that's enough," she said sharply.

"What's wrong ?" asked Barnaby, alarmed at her response.

"One of those names is not one we'd want to have anything to do with."

"But what is it ?" urged Barnaby. "Tell me."

"It's Beelzebub, lord of the flies. He was one of the most powerful and dangerous of all the demons. I've read about him," she said, averting her face. "Now I think we've looked enough at this book for now. Could you close it for me please ?"

Barnaby closed the book and placed it back inside the wallet. He had just returned it to his father's drawer when there was a long ring on the doorbell. They both jumped, still deep in the world of leather and demons and darkness. Barnaby went to the window and peered down.

"It's that verger," he hissed, his face animated. "He mustn't come in. Please! Don't let him come in!"

"I'll take care of it," said Helen. She shut the door and went downstairs.

A tall, dark haired man with an expressionless face stood at the door. Helen glanced briefly at his cassock.

"Oh. From the cathedral then ? How can I help you ?" she asked. Her tone was cool and business – like, but she felt afraid of this man. She didn't want to get near him, either, and she stepped back a pace. The verger smiled but something cold and calculating lurked in that smile. His face was deeply lined and his eyes steely blue.

"I would like to speak to Barnaby Abbott please."

He moved forward slightly and Helen recoiled. She couldn't help herself. His eyes narrowed.

"I'm afraid he's not well at the moment. He doesn't want any visitors."

"Perhaps I can help him," he said, still smiling fixedly at her.

"No thank you. I'm looking after him."

And with that she shut the door. Then she leaned against the wall, trembling.

The Dark Entry

CHAPTER ELEVEN

The man stood at Barnaby's door, his face black with anger and frustration. He raised his head, his eyes scanning the windows of the house. Sniffing the air, he caught the scent of an old familiar friend. He closed his eyes, then concentrated hard. The image of a leather bound book sharpened into focus. It was here – somewhere very close. He glimpsed a movement in the window of an upstairs room. *Ah, the boy, he has it.*

Things had not gone as he had planned. He could have taken the girl, but there had been something about her, some hidden strength, that had made him hesitate. She would come to regret slamming the door in his face. He knew how he would deal with her.

He strode away down the road towards the cathedral. After he had taken over the mind of the verger, his first instinct had been to enter but he realised the need for caution. He must discover the character of the body he had possessed. He must make no mistakes. If he was challenged he must be ready. He had earlier returned to the lodgings of his new host and found the place in a mess. His lip curled in contempt at the lack of self discipline and slovenly habits shown by this man. So this was how the world had progressed. He shuddered. There had been many modern objects which puzzled him but he had no interest in them. He was only concerned with gaining access to the cathedral, to the world he remembered from his own time.

He felt a thrill of excitement as the tall spire of the cathedral came into view. He stood in front of the Dark Entry for a moment and calmed his breathing. As he did so he became aware of the presence of others. Turning, he saw a small throng of sleek black creatures watching his every move.

The Dark Entry

His lips curved into a smile and he nodded his head in greeting to them. "Welcome my dark friends," he whispered. "Creatures of the night are we all. And well met. Now go, do your deed !"
The rats squealed and chattered in response, then turned and scattered.

*   *   *

The illness began the following day. The rats had spread everywhere, squeezing through open windows, basements, sewers, a relentless, dark tide of malice and corruption, infecting the young and the old, causing listlessness and fever in their wake. Some cried out in alarm as the rats emerged. Others chased them, beating at them with whatever came to hand. But the rats were fast and agile. As darkness fell, they spread further out into the city and beyond.

The first to be affected were those who lived closest to the cathedral. The very young were more susceptible. The initial symptom was that of a high temperature. This was then followed by swollen glands and nausea. Doctors were puzzled by the speed and severity of the symptoms. Suspecting that a virus was to blame, they recommended rest and mild analgesics, but as the symptoms worsened, they became concerned. The virus spread rapidly, stretching medical resources to the limits.

*   *   *

He gazed at the opening to the Dark Entry. He had already been shocked at the changes that had taken place since his own time – even when in the shambling body of the workman, he had felt despair and revulsion when confronted by the destruction of the old infirmary. He feared what else he

69

The Dark Entry

might find inside. He fingered the stonework of the wall with a sense of sorrow, mixed with anticipation and gazed up at a large wooden and glass structure. Where was the old library? What was this monstrosity perched in its place? His heart sank.

Earlier, he had noticed people seated at tables, eating and drinking. Clearly this was a hostry. It was not to his liking and had been given over to secular ways. But more importantly, what had become of his private chamber above the Dark Entry ? It had been his centre of power, his lodestone. He needed to find it.

Taking a deep breath, he entered the Dark Entry. He knew as he stood in the vaulted chamber that all trace of his own room had vanished. Despair and rage consumed him. The shock of being inside the cathedral precincts, an old familiar home, was unbearable.

Through the door he passed and found a large metal and glass box which reached up to the ceiling. There was no sign of the spiral staircase which once had given him access to his room. And where was the porter who kept his secrets and guarded his door ? And what had become of the access to the prior's lodging ? All had vanished utterly. The image of the dark and smoky room flooded his mind and he was overcome by a deep sense of loss. He could see the book-lined room with its flickering candlelight as if he had never left it. The smell of frankincense still clung to his nostrils. And there in the centre of the room was the grimoire and on it sat his only true friend, his familiar, a long, lean, supple black cat with emerald eyes. Shadow she was called, his dark messenger. She opened her mouth in a soundless mewl as if she saw him. Shadow. How he missed her. He felt a profound sense of loneliness and loss. And then the image vanished as quickly as it had come.

He calmed himself, aware of his rising panic. He would not give up so easily. He passed down the eastern cloister, noting that the building work had been completed. He glanced at Cloister Garth, an area of grassy silence. The summer light was fading fast but he glimpsed a pattern, surely, in the grass. What was that? He must find out.

70

The Dark Entry

Up on the roof bosses he could dimly make out small, carved figurines. He would need to return here in the morning when the light of day would illuminate them more clearly. But one particular carving caught his attention. It was of a man's face encased by luxuriant foliage. He sensed an older spirit here in this image and he felt the stirrings of the old dark magic rise within him.

Reaching the prior's door, he saw the fine doorway with its painted figures carved in an arch. He smiled, remembering them. Once inside the cathedral he paused and frowned. He had expected much change but not to this degree. Gone was the wooden roof. He stared up at the great fluted stone arches in amazement. The air inside was clean and smokeless. No rush lights burned. Instead there was some form of magical lighting with no apparent flame. He had puzzled over this in his lodgings and in the working man's home. Where once the monks would sit to pray and sing was now a series of carved seats. This must be where the boy would join his voice with others. Grand indeed were the seats, finely wrought and carved with strange fantastical figures. He stooped to examine them. There were angels, dragons, lions, eagles and several bearded, foliate men. The wodewose he recognised. These creatures belonged to the magic of nature, satyrs and fauns, yet they were here within the sacred precincts of the cathedral.

He sat quietly on one of the carved seats and rested for a while. Images returned, of robed monks, silent in prayer, their tonsured heads bowed in devotion. He could smell the smoke of the lights and the incense. He felt such a sense of loss that he cried out. He missed his position and influence.

He could almost touch the men, they were so real to him. The sound of voices shattered his vision and he slipped quietly out, back through the prior's door and out into the cloister. He would return to his own world and regain his power. It would not be an easy task but he must do it. And then…And then...

The Dark Entry

*   *   *

Back through the Dark Entry he passed, then stood looking at the few remains of the infirmary. He recalled the endless potions, both healing and magical, he had prepared here and how he had used the weak and the maimed for his experimentation. His porter had willingly disposed of those unfortunate enough to succumb to his ministrations. His fingers itched to be back at work. His agaric potion had been his most potent weapon, only to be used when the occasion demanded it. All those who gainsaid him had their dishes laced with it.

He noted his prior's lodging was still there. He would not see any more of these changes. He could not bear it. He turned away.

Barnaby's face sprang into his mind once more. A reminder to him that he had work to do. He would return to that dwelling, that old familiar house that he had purchased, away from the cathedral and its confines. He thought also of the woman who had kept his house, of her weakness and her betrayal. It was she who had hastened his end. She had kept the bastard child and reared it despite his efforts to locate her, but his power had begun to wane and he had failed.

All women were weak. They tempted men to their destruction. Women were there to be used and to be punished for Eve's original sin in the Garden of Eden. It did not occur to him, of course, that he had played a significant part in his own downfall and in his loss of celibacy. The flame haired girl who had barred his entry to the house was one of the daughters of Eve. She too was cursed, just like all the others.

He would visit the house when the boy was away. He would find his book, his treasure, his power and he would reawaken his ambition and quest. He would create such magic in this modern age that the world would quake with fear. He would take his power. In the end he would triumph.

CHAPTER TWELVE

The following morning Le Prevost rang the bell and waited. A small, rounded woman with short dark hair and glasses opened the door. She noted his cassock and smiled politely.

"Good morning, Mrs Abbott. I'm terribly sorry to disturb you." He smiled unctuously and shook her hand.

"Oh that's alright," replied Sarah, noting how cold and clammy his hand was. "How can I help you ?"

"It's about your son, Barnaby. May I come in ?"

"Oh yes, of course. There's nothing wrong, I hope ?" she said anxiously.

"No, no. Don't worry. Nothing to be alarmed about, I assure you."

Le Prevost was reassuring and kindly. He smiled, yet his eyes noted every object within the hallway. The house had changed utterly. It was as if he had never been in this house before, it was so different. In his time the house had been darker and the wood panelled. But the place was now strangely different. It was lighter and seemed barer by comparison. Gone were the old wall paintings, the wainscotting, the tapestries and the great open fireplace. Yet, though he mourned their passing, he needed to move on. He needed to find the book.

"Do come into the library. I'm afraid my husband's at work."

"What exactly is your husband's work ?" asked Le Prevost.

"He's a scientist of sorts. He's very busy at the moment. Actually, he's involved with the discovery of the coffin in the grounds of the cathedral."

Le Prevost stiffened slightly, then nodded.

"Yes, an interesting case," he remarked. His voice seemed colder somehow. "I expect he has discovered much of interest." There was a pause, then he spoke again. "Tell me, the coffin, were there ancient relics within ?"

What an odd turn of phrase, thought Sarah.

The Dark Entry

"Well, yes there were. They're working on them at the moment."

"These relics. Where would they be kept ?"

Le Prevost leaned forward. His gaze was fixed upon Sarah so intently that she felt trapped by his presence.

"Well, er, mostly at the university."

"I see," said Le Prevost. He leaned back and studied her. She was lying, he knew, but he *would* find his grimoire.

"Well. What did you want to say about Barnaby ?" Sarah asked faintly.

"Ah." Le Prevost smiled benignly. "The choir master asked me to have a word with you. It is not in my remit, of course, but I knew he was concerned. Your child, it seems, has been acting rather strangely of late. Withdrawn and secretive as if he were affected by something."

"Oh, really. Well, he has looked very pale and a little unhappy, I have to admit. Look, would you like a drink ? Sorry, but I didn't actually catch your name ?"

"Water would be most acceptable," replied Le Prevost. "I should have introduced myself, dear lady. How very uncouth of me. My name is Peter Cotton and I am a verger at the cathedral."

Sarah excused herself and left the room. She felt strangely odd, she didn't know why. The verger had had a curious effect on her.

In the study Le Prevost closed his eyes and pictured the leather bound grimoire. He knew it had to be here. He could sense it. He and the book were as one. He moved to the desk, hovering like a bird of prey, then he conjured it in his mind's eye. Ah, there it was, below him, in a drawer of the desk. He uttered words of power under his breath and there, before him, the drawer slid open, slowly and silently. Inside, he saw a package and leaning down, he pulled it gently from the drawer. He removed the strange material of the packaging. Taking a tome from the bookshelf, he placed it inside the wallet and returned it to the drawer. His grimoire was somewhat bulky but he concealed it under his cassock. Then he found Sarah in the kitchen.

"I am most terribly sorry, but I find I am late for an appointment with the bishop. We must talk again about Barnaby, Mrs Abbott. Perhaps at a future date. Many thanks."

The Dark Entry

Sarah was surprised at the abruptness of his departure, but inwardly relieved at his going. He had made her feel most uncomfortable. She closed the door behind him and breathed a sigh of relief but a chill remained with her throughout that morning. And then she thought of Barnaby. What on earth was troubling him ?

*   *   *

Barnaby was the last to leave school. He passed through the Dark Entry. There was no longer the feeling of dread that had virtually paralysed him before and he hadn't seen the verger recently. Well, thank goodness for that, he thought.

"Hey Barnaby, how ya doing ?"
Barnaby turned and smiled. It was Luke. His sun-bleached hair had grown over the holidays, contrasting with his tanned face.
"Luke !" cried Barnaby. How are you ?"
"I'm good. How are you, though ?"
"I'm feeling better about this place," replied Barnaby as he switched his gaze to the Dark Entry. "Darren helped me."
"Oh, that's good. It's been great that we've all been able to spend time together."
"Yes. I've really enjoyed it. I like Darren. He's cool. I've something to tell you though – it's not so good. How about some tea at my place ?"

Luke was struck by the sudden change of mood in Barnaby, so he smiled warmly and agreed, trying to be supportive.
"Yeah. That's just what I need now. Come on. Let's get out of here."
They walked back to Barnaby's house deep in conversation. Barnaby explained all that had happened to him and Darren and Helen. Luke became concerned when he heard about the verger.

The Dark Entry

"That's not good," he said quietly. "You'll need to take care in the cathedral then."

"Do you think so ?" asked Barnaby.

"Yes. I just have a feeling, that's all. Things have been so strange lately. Look what happened to me down by the river."

"What happened to you ?"

Barnaby's voice rose in concern.

"I was attacked for no reason. Everyone seems so aggressive, violent even. I don't like it, and I don't like the way I responded either. But never mind all that. I still haven't taken you to Cromer yet. We'll go there and chill out as soon as we can. Need to get the surf right first though. What about it, Barnaby ?"

When Barnaby opened the front door he heard his mother call from upstairs. Her voice was faint.

"Luke, go and make yourself comfortable. I won't be a minute," he said.

He found his mother propped up in bed, her face flushed and her breathing heavy.

"Oh Barnaby. There you are. I'm so glad you're back. I feel so ill. I felt alright and then the verger came and he was asking me questions and…I just felt so weak afterwards."

Barnaby felt a sudden chill sweep through him.

"The verger ? What was he doing here ?" His voice was shrill and his face pale.

"He was concerned about you. About how you'd been lately."

"Why ? He doesn't know me. Did you ask him in ?"

"Yes. I didn't much like him. He made me feel really uncomfortable. Now. You'll have to make your own tea. Tell Luke I'm sorry. I want to sleep now."

Barnaby walked downstairs, his thoughts in turmoil. Why was his mother so ill ? She looked awful. Had the verger done something to her ? For the first time he felt real anger rise in him. How dare this man hurt his mother ! He found the surgery number in his mother's address book and rang it. They said they would send a locum out later on, but they had been inundated with emergencies.

Barnaby pushed his plate away.

"I can't finish this. I can't get him out of my head, Luke and I'm really worried about mum."

"Don't let it get to you," said Luke. "I'll stay for a while. If there's anything I can do... And if you don't want the rest of your beans, I'll have them."

He laughed and grinned. Barnaby relaxed a little. Luke was such good company, especially in a crisis.

They chatted for a while but Barnaby's thoughts were elsewhere. He kept thinking of the verger in their house. Somehow the place felt tainted by his presence. This spirit, this creature that was Le Prevost had returned to his old haunts. What would he do ? Had he done his dark deeds here ? Is that why his visions had been so clear ? Was he going to reclaim the house as his ? He wondered if he had hidden magical objects in the fabric of the building. His blood ran cold at the thought of it. This was Barnaby's sanctuary. But was he still safe here ?

Then a thought struck him. The grimoire. Would he have searched for it ? He ran into the study, panic seizing hold of him. He must have sensed where it was. Were his powers getting stronger ?

"Luke. Come quick. The grimoire, he must have come for it."

"What grimoire ?" asked Luke.

"You know, the book I told you about. The book I opened and Helen and I read some of it."

Luke raced into the study to find Barnaby kneeling by the drawer of a large writing desk. His face was contorted, his eyes staring.

"It's gone," he whispered, appalled, his hands shaking. "He found it. We're done for."

There was a prolonged silence. Luke sat on the sofa and looked at Barnaby.

The Dark Entry

"Get the others," he said firmly. "Call them. They need to be here."

CHAPTER THIRTEEN

Luke paced up and down the study, restlessly waiting for Darren and Helen to arrive. Upstairs, Barnaby was sitting with his mother, watching her as she slept. Luke went from room to room, touching the old, irregular walls. He put his ear to the wall of the study and closed his eyes. He heard the creak of timber and smelt an underlying dank odour and wondered if there had been a spring or an old well nearby. He had such an affinity with water he could dowse a place without divining rods. He could smell it and almost taste it. What untold stories lay here in this house ? What things lay hidden behind this wall ?

He roamed the house, touching and listening as he went. He came to Barnaby's mother's room. She was deep in sleep, hot with fever, face glistening with sweat while Barnaby dozed in the chair beside her. He looked done in. Softly, quietly, Luke went to the wall and listened. At first there was nothing, then a slight scratching began beneath the skirting board. He lay on the floor, pressing his ear as close as possible to the surface of the wood. There it was again. This time louder and more urgent. Rats ! He knew they were abroad in large numbers. He had seen them, not only by the river, but up in the city. He tapped sharply on the wood. The noise ceased momentarily, then resumed once more. He went over and quietly spoke to Barnaby.

"Barnaby. There are rats here," he whispered. "They're everywhere in the area. Haven't you noticed ?"

"Yes. I saw some this morning," said Barnaby. "Near the Dark Entry. Do you think they have anything to do with *him* ?"

"Sounds a bit far – fetched, but you may be onto something," replied Luke.

They tiptoed out of the room, then went to wait for the others.

80

The Dark Entry

"I hope you don't mind me bringing my mother, Barnaby," said Helen. "She really wants to help. I've told her everything, and I mean EVERYTHING, including the stuff about the verger."

Barnaby was relieved to see Anne. He remembered her strength and courage when they had been threatened. If anyone could help it would be her. And it was good to have Darren here, too.

"I'm really glad to see you, Mrs Murray. Mum's not at all well. We think it's...him..."
"Don't worry, Barnaby." Anne smiled warmly at him. "I'll do what I can."
Barnaby gazed up at her. She was tall, like her daughter, with the same green eyes, but with rich auburn hair, tinged with occasional grey. That must be where Helen gets her looks from, he thought.

Anne strode around each room. She paused occasionally as if to listen.
"Show me your mother's room, please, Barnaby," she said briskly.
They all went upstairs and stood quietly outside Sarah's room. She was still deep in her fever, her breathing slow and laboured. They waited while Anne entered the room. She went over to the bed and placed her hand upon Sarah's forehead. There was a silence as she stood, eyes closed in concentration. Then she began to murmur. To Barnaby's ears it sounded almost like a chant, and surely his mother's breathing had eased a little ? She stepped back, away from the bed, and then made her way round the room, listening at each wall. Suddenly she stopped.

"Ah," she breathed. "I'll have you."
The others looked at each other in surprise. Helen smiled at them.
"She's good, you know. She knows what she's doing. Remember ?"
Indeed Darren *did* remember the events in Helen's house. It seemed such a long time ago but much had happened since. He pushed away the image of his father's tortured form and the fight they had endured together.

The Dark Entry

Anne turned and beckoned to her daughter.

"Helen. Come here," she said in a quiet voice. She did not want Sarah to waken. She might be afraid of a strange woman in her room. Helen and Anne stood side by side, facing the wall.

"Now. Remember what I've taught you, Helen. Concentrate hard and follow my lead."

They linked hands and Anne drew a small ash stick from her skirt pocket. Darren shifted uneasily. It looked suspiciously like a wand to him. She pointed the stick at the wall and began to sing her spell. It was a quiet, slightly unearthly sound.

Soon Helen joined her. To her surprise, and without any warning, she felt someone move beside her. Turning, she saw Luke's tanned face, suddenly serious. He took her hand and began to hum. Something deep within him had responded to this ancient sound and he found himself drawn to it, unable to resist.

The three stood there, hands locked, ash stick now pressing against the wall and it seemed to the two watching that the three had become as one. The light shimmered around them as the sound deepened and became more resonant. Still the sleeping woman slumbered on, unaware of the room and its occupants. So the power grew and Anne's voice rose. The sounds from behind the wall became more frantic and insistent. Again the voices grew and the words that Anne uttered had no meaning for Barnaby, but he sensed the strength that lay behind them. Helen's voice joined that of her mother, a higher, purer sound while Luke's deep hum grounded them both. As the spell reached a crescendo, Anne struck the wall three times in succession, shouting: "OUT ! OUT ! OUT !" Helen and Luke responded and the room was filled with the strident cadence of voices. There was one final screech from behind the wall and then the voices fell silent.

Complete stillness now and the quiet of the room slowly began to calm their senses.

The Dark Entry

"They've gone !" said Luke. "I can hear nothing now. Nothing at all." He gazed at Anne in wonder.

"Barnaby, come in," called Anne.

Barnaby ran to his mother. She was still deep in sleep but the fever had lessened.

"Her breathing's easier," he said, in amazement. "Whatever you've done, thank you." As he turned to the three by the wall, Anne slowly shook herself, then spoke.

"She's not out of the woods yet, Barnaby. She needs to rest. She needs to sleep and regain her strength." Anne went to Sarah's side and slid a small bundle of herbs under her pillow.

"Bay leaves and rosemary. They'll keep her safe." Then she drew a small bottle from her pocket. "This will also help her. Give her three drops in some water, three times a day." She handed the mixture to Barnaby. "Now, let's give her some peace."

* * *

Anne drank her tea gratefully.

"Oh, this is welcome," she said. "Thanks Barnaby. Now, hopefully the little devils will stay away. If you have any more trouble with them, call me. But there is a heaviness about this house. I can almost taste it. There's a darkness here from the past, trapped in the fabric of the place. I haven't forgotten the room over the Dark Entry by the way. Tomorrow, when I visit the record office, I hope to be able to find out precisely whether there was a room and if so, who used it. Now, I'd just like to relax for a while."

Barnaby switched on the television, then lounged on the floor, elbows under his chin.

"Oh, it's only the local news," he said in a disappointed voice, but as they sat and relaxed, chatting, they were interrupted by Darren's sharp voice.

The Dark Entry

"Hey. Hold on! Listen." As they watched, a reporter began to speak on camera.

"The mysterious illness is spreading rapidly and appears to be reaching epidemic proportions."

"Look," exclaimed Helen, "he's standing outside Erpingham Gate. He's down by the cathedral ! It all comes from there !"

The reporter continued:

"So many people have now been affected that the Norwich Hospital has had to divert admissions to other areas. As yet, no one has been able to identify the virus but the health authorities and the police have been inundated with sightings of rats. No one can explain why there has been such an explosion in their numbers. Possible concern about their appearance followed by the sickness has reached an alarming level in the city and there has even been a suggestion of plague. The authorities are asking anyone who feels the onset of fever to remain inside. Bed rest and plenty of liquids are the recommended treatment."

The camera panned away from the reporter, taking in the cathedral and its environs.

"Oh, please turn it off !" cried Helen. "This is awful ! It's like the bubonic plague all over again ! It's happened before and now it's happening again. It's no coincidence that these things have been happening since that blessed coffin was opened. We've got to stop him."

"Yes, " said Barnaby quietly, "and he was here. Le Prevost. In this house. I haven't had time to tell you all, what with my mum and everything, but now he was here and the grimoire is missing."

There was a stunned silence.

CHAPTER FOURTEEN

Le Prevost laid the grimoire carefully on the kitchen table. He sat and gazed at the old, familiar, leather-bound book that contained so many of his secrets. If he was to return to his power base, he needed to travel, through past centuries, back into the time before his demise. Time to tap into that immense dark power he had built up so carefully over the years. He smiled thinly as he thought of the efforts of these modern humans to gain access to his spells.

With long, bony fingers, he gently prised open the brass hasp and opened the book. He knew at once that someone else had accessed the grimoire. He could smell a presence. Who could it have been ? He frowned in anger. No one had the power to do this except him. He closed his eyes and focussed his thoughts on the book. Slowly the image intensified. He could see the book quite clearly on a table. A hand moved into view, slowly opening the hasp. He caught his breath in amazement. A young hand! The boy!

The picture moved outwards and there he saw Barnaby, face flushed with triumph as he slowly turned the page. He spoke to someone beyond Le Prevost's vision. He cursed loudly. What was this ? How could the boy be the only other one to access his most sacred of books ? He thought of the woman in his own time. She who should have known better. She who had betrayed him, who had been with child. Surely she had found the means to destroy the unborn one ? But he knew. The feeling was too strong. He knew now why this boy was special, why he had been so drawn to him. He was of his own flesh and blood. Down through the years his blood line had been clearly preserved and survived. For the first time his hatred of the woman diminished a little. She had done him a great favour. Now at last he knew what he must do with the boy, but first he must find his spell.

The Dark Entry

Memories flooded back as he sought the page. He found his mind was plunged into the past. He saw for the first time the woman, cloaked and hooded, holding a newly born child. Then dark, smoky memories filled with rabid faces, stretched wide in anger and fear. The clamour of shouting, hateful voices filled his head and he saw himself running in a wild panic, running for his life. Running through and out of the cathedral with the mob hot in pursuit. Flaming torches flared, mocking and taunting him. He felt the thud of a missile, a stone perhaps, as it cracked into his back. Turning, he stopped, drew forth his black wand and pointed it at them. They struggled and stopped in their tracks, slipping and falling in their haste and fear. Le Prevost cursed them loudly, then ran on.

Yet still they pursued him – along Ferry Lane and round over the bridge and up to the hill. Then the vision vanished and he held his head in his hands, moaning softly. He ached to be back there, up in his secret chamber. Then he would show them what he could do and the darkness he would unleash upon them.

He needed to obtain the means by which he could return in physical form to his own time. The time before his inquisition by the Star Chamber and his subsequent death at the hands of the mob. He would avenge himself against the stinking rabble of the city, those who had dared to lay hands on him. This would never happen again. He would see to it. He would make himself invincible. *No, immortal.* Ambition laced with malice welled up in him like a molten river. He could see their faces, even now, twisted with hatred and red with the lust of the chase.

Hidden under the floorboards in the centre of the room above the Dark Entry was a glass phial he had carefully concealed. This was his centre of power, his locus of operations, acquired through long and painful years of intense ritual and study in the dark arts. It contained the essence of his creature, bound and confined by his magical spells. If only he could but retrieve it and use it with the words of power from the grimoire for the Great Ritual…

But for now – a spell to subdue the present world and bring it to heel. Something to bring him enjoyment in this wretched sphere. He drank

86

some water and ran his hand through his hair – an old calming gesture he had forgotten. It brought him back into this world, into his senses, and he continued to leaf through the grimoire once more.

One page caught his eye. It was an old familiar spell. One to bring forth water. Water in torrents and spates that would flood forth and cleanse the land, ridding it of unwanted pious energies. He would show modern man what real power could do.

He closed his eyes once more, steepling his fingers into the very shape of the spire of the building he had grown to detest, the place that had brought about his downfall. He felt some of his old power begin to grow. It spread up from the earth, through the floor, up into his legs and through his torso until he shivered and tingled with the thrill of it. Opening his eyes, he traced the intricate pattern on the page in front of him, mouthing quiet words of dark magic that began to rise and fill the air above his head, forming a dark cloud and hovering over him, waiting. He spoke the words of power and then blew away the dark cloud with one huge breath. It lifted and turned and was gone, seeping through the window and out into the world, where it thickened and spread and darkened with menace. Turning away from the window, Le Prevost smiled as he heard the first few drops of rain fall.

*   *   *

And the cloud moved swiftly over the city streets. People looked up into the sky as the early evening light was blotted out and they shivered apprehensively. On it travelled to where Helen was sitting on the floor of her lounge, her mother close beside her, holding her hand, talking earnestly. Occult books and papers were spread around them while Helen listened intently to her mother's wise teaching. They both paused suddenly as the first drops of rain rattled down the windows and sank into the earth.

The Dark Entry

*   *   *

And Luke gazed up at the ominous cloud as he packed away his fishing tackle at the Ferry. He sniffed the air, smelling the strange, dank odour. There was no sound at all here. All birds and creatures had fled, down into their holes, into bushes and trees and under the eaves of houses. Luke's flesh tingled as he sensed an otherworldly presence rise like a dank mist. As he made his way up towards the cathedral, the rain began to fall, lightly at first. Then heavily, beating down hard on his head and shoulders. Soon there was a stream of water rushing down towards the Ferry. He began to run.

*   *   *

The cloud moved swiftly now, passing over the house where Darren and his parents were enjoying their evening meal in companionable silence. They stirred, glancing at the window nervously as the sky darkened. Darren went to the window and stared in disbelief as the heavens opened and the rain began to pound the streets and houses. His father came to stand beside him and watched in silence as the rain started to flood the gutters, putting a reassuring hand on Darren's shoulder as if remembering some recent dark dream. He shuddered.

*   *   *

The Dark Entry

The cloud paused, hovering over Barnaby's house, thickening and intensifying in density. And as the rain fell, Barnaby gave his mother tea and propped up her pillow and she smiled weakly, thanking him. His father's anger reflected the blackness of the sky as he stood, hands on hips, berating his son. Perhaps he had found the empty drawer in the desk, perhaps he was angry at the invasion of so many visitors when his wife was so ill. They all stopped, turning to stare through the window as the rain lashed down heavily as if trying to beat its way into the house.

*   *   *

And the rain continues and the black cloud grows ever larger, the colour of pitch now, hanging over the city roofs. The torrent pushes its way through the gutters, sluicing down drainpipes, cascading down into cellars. So the floods begin to rise and the streets become swollen rivers, swirling the dross of human life before it.

And the dark waters breach the cathedral and its environs, submerging gardens, swirling through houses as desperate residents scramble for safety. Higher and higher it rises, bursting through the great oak doors of the cathedral, surging like a wild horse down the centre of the nave, scattering pews and prayer books in its wake. So it continues, beyond the precincts, down to the court house and on until the two great forces of rain and river meet in a wild, unstoppable roar.

And still the sky darkens.

And from his lodgings the cowled verger passes swiftly through the streets and across the city to the great concrete monolith of the university. He stands in the rain, eyes closed, mind focussing on his missing past. The

The Dark Entry

magic is stronger now. He sees them in the tall building to his left. He stifles his revulsion at the sight of this drab, alien landscape, then moves quickly and quietly up the steps. No one sees him. The door is locked but he opens it with ease. A figure moves inside and is stilled by a word. The verger scans the room and there, in a box in the corner, he finds his ring, his serpent ring with its jet-like stone. There is no trace of his other possessions. He places the ring on his middle finger and feels his energy intensify. He leaves the building, unseen.

The Dark Entry

CHAPTER FIFTEEN

Still the rain fell, but less heavily now. Firemen and volunteers could be seen evacuating residents from their houses as far up as the Lower Close. The lower areas of the houses and offices were filled with flood water mixed with sewage, which left a noxious smell.

Luke joined the army of volunteers and spent some hours in the cleaning up operations. He waded down to the Ferry, checking the houses as he went. He was concerned about the wildlife on and around the river. As he drew closer, he could see several distressed ducks and swans and in the rain-beaten branches of trees huddled wet, miserable birds. The ducks protested angrily at him as if he were responsible for what had happened. He crooned softly, a reassuring sound and gradually they calmed down. He was distressed to see the damage done at the height of the flood. Much vegetation had been snapped and uprooted and the River Wensum was filled with debris. Although the waters had dropped slightly, the current was still very strong.

His gaze was caught by a small brown shape struggling in the water. It was a dog, its head dipping below the surface, then re-emerging. It was very tired and he knew he must act quickly. Wrenching off his heavy waders, he paddled to the river's edge and dived in. The water was deathly cold, much colder than the sea at Cromer where he surfed. This was unnatural for the time of year. And it reeked.

He kept his mouth shut to avoid contamination. The water swirled around him as he forced his way out to the dog. I have little time left, he thought frantically as the dog disappeared once more. He took a deep breath, then dived into the swirling, murky depths. He could barely see through the churned mud and tangle of driftwood but at last he spotted the small creature. His years of swimming and surfing had served him well,

The Dark Entry

had strengthened his body. With one last powerful spurt he grabbed it by the scruff of its neck and forced his way up to the surface. He fought against the current as he gripped the frantic dog and when he finally reached the bank, he struggled out of the waters, then released the dog onto the towpath. The dog shook itself fiercely, then trotted off away from the river. What a foolish boy you are, putting yourself at risk, he could almost hear his mother say. But he could not have stood and watched the dog drown, whatever the risk. It was not in his nature.

Panting with fatigue, he leaned against an old willow tree. His head was spinning and he found it hard to focus. The world spun around him as he struggled up the path. He looked back at the river and for a moment his vision blurred. The light shimmered on the water's surface, dazzling him.

It was then the shapes appeared, subtly at first, then gathering form and substance. What were they ? He rubbed his eyes and looked again, but they were still there. Fish - like shapes, diving and plunging, playing like dolphins. Soft, sinuous creatures, rising and falling with the motion of the water. Enchanted, he lost all sense of reality and began to move towards them. One shape shifted closer. It had the form of a fish and yet he could have sworn he saw tresses of dark hair floating around it.

It began to sing a soft, haunting melody, hypnotic and alluring. He could not resist its call. As he drew closer he could see the shape of a human face with soft, penetrating eyes. Was this a mermaid ? The figure beckoned, smiling wistfully at him. The eyes were green and translucent, the flesh soft and rounded, enticing him to join her. Luke was filled with a strange rapture. At that moment nothing else mattered. All thoughts of Helen, Darren, Barnaby and Le Prevost vanished and the moment became an eternity. He was filled with the vision of her and in her song he heard his name and felt her longing. And then the song became more insistent, haunting in its refrain.

As he neared the bank he held out his arms towards the creature, unable to resist its call. As he did so, he heard a sudden flapping of wings and felt an intense pain sear through his arm. There followed a loud screech. He could see taloned claws gripping his outstretched forearm.

92

The Dark Entry

Dazed, he staggered back and there, staring fixedly at him, was a small, white owl. It was a barn owl and he could feel its unwavering urgency. It clasped his arm for a few seconds, waking him from his trance, then flew away, leaving blood streaming from him. Shaking himself in astonishment, he looked back at the river, wondering why the creature had attacked him.

The alluring, seductive entities began to alter and shift. Slowly and subtly, the dolphin-like forms darkened and sharpened into focus. Now he could see jagged teeth and cruel eyes and he retreated. The song of the mermaid shifted into a shrill, shrieking sound, so loud and penetrating that he thought his ears would burst. He staggered back on the bank, slipping and sliding in the mud and water as the shapes advanced. All he could see now were eyes and teeth and he felt afraid.

He stilled his mind, then called to them, but the shrieking was all consuming. There was no communication to be had. As they drew close, he felt despair overwhelm him. He had no way of knowing whether these shapes were real or a fantasy he had dreamt up in his exhausted state. He clutched the leather thong of his amulet in desperation. It was an automatic action and he could see Helen's mother in his mind as his hand slipped down the cord and grasped the runic stone she had given him.

It was the rune of water and of earth. It gave him strength and he stood upright once more, the warmth of the stone growing fast into a glimmer of light. So the light grew stronger and shone like a beacon. He released the stone and still it shone brighter than before.

Taking it from around his neck, he held it high and it beamed out, rays of light piercing the darkness of the water. Words came to him and he spoke without thinking.

"Get back to your dark master where you belong! Back! Back!"

The shapes reared up, twisting and writhing but as the light touched them, they began to shrink and distort. What Luke had thought was a mermaid became a black, ugly seething mass of hatred. It keened and

93

moaned as it shrank. He watched in mounting horror, each of the shapes slowly dwindling and retreating.

He blinked in amazement. What were they? What had the verger conjured up? He moved to the edge of the bank, the light beaming before him. He peered down into the murky depths. And so it was that he saw the shapes dwindle into a bedraggled collection of rats. Large black rats that had appeared so recently. He knew their origin. They screamed their defiance at him as the light continued to shine, then turned and swam in a pack upstream.

Luke began to shake with the cold and shock. He felt numb and exhausted.

*   *   *

Helen, Darren and Barnaby lounged in the leather sofas of the Forum café, chatting idly.

"Mum should be here by now," said Helen impatiently. "She's always late ! But how's your mum now, Barnaby ? Tell us all."

"She's really getting better," said Barnaby. He was more relaxed and cheerful now. "I think your mother really helped her, Helen. But my father still thinks I took the grimoire."

As he spoke, Anne appeared, flustered and dishevelled. Barnaby thought how much she and Helen looked alike. Even the clothes were similar. Quite hippyish he thought. Lots of bright colours and different layers.

"I'm so sorry I'm late," said Anne. "I got caught in the traffic. It's a nightmare trying to park. I managed to get into St Andrews car park. Anyway, I hope Sarah is improving, Barnaby ? Have the herbs helped ?"

"Oh yes, thank you. She's heaps better."

The Dark Entry

"And how are you, Darren ?" she asked.

"I'm okay. Things have been weird lately, haven't they ? People are so angry and aggressive."

"Where's Luke ?" asked Anne, glancing round.

"Well, I tried to ring him," said Helen. "No answer I'm afraid, so I left a message. Hope he gets here. But what have you got for us, mum ?"

Anne opened her shoulder bag and dug out a folder.

"I found some documents in the record office. I've managed to get photocopies. The original was in Latin but fortunately someone had provided a translation. This is the gist of it. Well, Barnaby, you were right about the room above the Dark Entry. It certainly did exist. We know that it was Le Prevost in the tomb, don't we ?"

They all nodded.

"Well, we now know that he also had access to that room. In fact, he had a porter whose job it was to guard the entrance and make sure that all visitors were vetted before entering. I imagine the prior would want to maintain his privacy. What is now clear is that Le Prevost was, in fact, the prior – a man of great importance."

Helen looked thoughtful.

"So he was very powerful. I see." She looked somewhat worried. "He might be more dangerous than we thought."

"Well, you've learned a lot, Helen. You're strong in your own power." Darren shifted uncomfortably. Talk of power and magic still made him feel uneasy and a little afraid.

"Well there's more," continued Anne. "What we also know is that after his trial the local people rose up against him. He had treated them very badly and was cruel to a good many of them. Fortunately I don't have all the details. I think I'd rather not know."

Helen nodded in agreement.

"Anyway, they got together a large mob and overran the cathedral, doing a great deal of damage, then hunted him down." The three leaned forward, fascinated. "They chased him out of the cathedral precincts, but there's no record of what happened next."

"Oh damn !" said Darren loudly. "Now we'll never know."

The Dark Entry

"No, but as you know he was buried in a lead coffin with most of his artefacts. I think the lead was meant to prevent his spirit from escaping."

"Oh," said Darren. "And then my dad punctured it. It's his fault."

"No," said Anne, firmly. "He couldn't have known it was there, could he? You mustn't blame him. He's been through enough already."

"Okay," said Darren. "I know."

"I'll try to find out about the other things that were in the coffin," said Barnaby, "if that's any use."

"Well, yes, it may well be," replied Anne. "In fact I think –"

She was interrupted by Barnaby's shout.

"God ! What's happened to you ?"

There, in front of them, stood the damp, bedraggled form of Luke.

He was shaking.

CHAPTER SIXTEEN

"**W**hat on earth has happened ?" asked Anne . "You look terrible. Come and sit down, Luke. Helen fetch him a coffee. A strong one."

Luke sat and sipped his coffee gratefully. Darren put his jacket round Luke's sopping shoulders.
"You need to dry out. Tell us what happened."
Luke paused for a moment, remembering the vision, then began his story. When he had finished, Darren whistled under his breath.
"God ! Weird !"
"The rats – they must have been sent by him," said Helen. "He's getting stronger all the time. We need to stick together. Especially now he has the grimoire. What will he try to do next ?"
Anne shook her head.
"It's hard to say. We don't know his intent. Nor how skilful he might be as a magician. Will he have the same powers that he once had, when he was alive? There's no way of knowing. But we need to be prepared for anything. I have to go now but, all of you, stay together as much as possible and always wear your amulets!"

She kissed Helen and left.

"Well I'm glad I wore my amulet," said Luke. "Under the circumstances I don't know what would have happened. Anyway, I feel exhausted. I need to get home now. Take a shower. My mother will wonder what's been going on."
"I'll come with you," said Darren. "Just to keep an eye on you – that's all. I'd like to meet your mum."

The Dark Entry

Helen stood and gazed out at the sky.

"It's stopping," she said. "Look. The sky's brightening. Come on Barnaby. I'll walk home with you. Keep in touch everyone."

*   *   *

Through the whole of that night the flood waters slowly ebbed, leaving a trail of litter and silt-blocked drains. Some areas of the city remained under water where sewers and gutters had been completely blocked. In other places, water had seeped back down into the earth, leaving thick layers of mud, polluted with sewage and the detritus of human life. Plastic bags and polystyrene containers from fast food outlets mingled with overturned supermarket trolleys and abandoned cars. And the stench was everywhere.

In the Close itself, residents stood in their houses staring in despair at the wreckage of their lives. Encrusted furniture, thrown higgledy piggledy by the force of the waters, precious photographs of loved ones peering from the silt, a wide screen TV lying awkwardly across a windowsill. All had to be dealt with.

At nine o'clock sharp, breakfasted and suitably dressed, Barnaby left the house. His Wellington boots were a little small, pinching his feet, and his waterproofs made him sweat and look like a nerd, but nevertheless he was determined to help the clear up operation at the cathedral. He needed to occupy his mind – something to take away the feeling of agitation he felt. He was very pleased that his mother was recovering so quickly but she had revealed some disturbing information. Before she was ill she had photocopied some documents from the record office concerning the house but had not been able to follow them up. He had taken her briefcase to her in the study and she had read through the papers with a quiet absorption. Then she had told him the very news he had not wanted to hear.

The Dark Entry

Le Prevost was a direct ancestor from his father's side of the family. It had been tortuous and difficult to trace the ancestry forward in time. Le Prevost had fathered an illegitimate son, the mother of whom had testified against him in the Star Chamber. After his death and burial in the lead coffin outside the immediate precincts of the cathedral, she had been offered some charity by the church authorities and had been married off to a local wheelwright, Josiah Abbott, who had brought up the child as his own flesh and blood. Sarah had been struck by the name and had traced the lineage of the Abbott family through the centuries. Once she had the bit between her teeth it was impossible to stop her. At first she had found the coincidence of the house and the ancestor surprising and rather amusing, but when she had seen Barnaby's reaction she felt some sympathy for him and had reassured him that this disreputable man had lived a long time ago.

When he arrived at the cathedral, Barnaby was told by a security guard in no uncertain terms that he would NOT be allowed to help for reasons of health and safety and that it was more than his job was worth to let him in. But when the man's back was turned, Barnaby slipped round to the entrance of the shop and peered in. There was a team of people inside, wearing protective clothing, peering down into the mud. They were removing piles of sodden books and goods from the thin layer of mud, methodically placing them in plastic boxes outside.

Barnaby retreated and found a damp seat, away from the action. He could hardly believe he could be a descendant of that vile creature. How extraordinary to think he could have been the prior of the cathedral, yet at the same time could have wielded such a malign influence. It didn't make any sense at all. And what about his own personality? Did he have the same potential for such evil? He hoped not.

He moved restlessly onwards, seeking the herbarium and turned back towards the Dark Entry. The security man was still there! Damn it, he thought. And as he wondered what to do, he saw a figure emerge from the Dark Entry. It was the verger, or Le Prevost, as he would now call him. At the same time the security officer spotted Barnaby and shouted.

"Hey ! I told you to clear off ! I mean it ! Now... get lost !"

99

The Dark Entry

Le Prevost turned to see who the man was addressing and saw Barnaby. His eyes gleamed and he started to move towards him. Barnaby ran as best he could through the silt and debris from the flood and soon disappeared from view.

Le Prevost watched him leave, then turned back.
"Little sod !" said the security man, "if you'll pardon my French sir."
Le Prevost smiled thinly, then made his way around the corner towards the deanery. This was where he had lodged in former times. His head hurt with a sudden sharp pain and he leant against the ancient wall for support, his mind full of painful memories.

His head was awash with smoke and incense as he was plunged back through time. He could see the dim outline of the High Altar and there, in front of it, stood the bishop, his face stern and forbidding. He recalled the words of the exorcism as if they had been uttered only yesterday. He fought against the vivid memory but snatches of the oration drifted through.

"Depart then transgressor, full of lies and cunning, persecutor of the innocent."
His lips drew back into a snarl of anger. How dare they !
"Give way, you monster, give way to Christ... He has cast you forth into the outer darkness..."
And so it continued and so he fought against it.
"Asp, basilisk, lion and dragon, depart from this man..."

He felt a roar surge up in his throat but clamped it down hard. He must not draw attention to himself. They had taken him to the Dark Entry and repeated certain words and phrases again, and then he had been cast out, unceremoniously thrown, like a piece of baggage, from the door. The rioters were outside, waiting for him, banging on the door. He roared an unearthly challenge at them and had slipped past before they even knew it.
"We almost had him !" one of the rabble had shouted.

He had started his ritual, high up on the hill, but still they had found him.

The Dark Entry

The pain had not lasted long.

He came to abruptly. He was shaking and cold and the security officer was standing staring down at him.

"Alright sir ? Need any help ?"

Le Prevost shook his head vehemently.

"No…no… All is well. Thank you," he said. And he turned and walked slowly away. He needed desperately to get back to the time before the exorcism. He would change the course of events, re-establish his authority. But how would he do it ? Of that he was not sure.

Back at the verger's lodgings, in the silence, he sipped at a glass of red wine and sat in silence, gathering his strength. Then he opened the grimoire and turned the pages carefully. Spells to conjure up elementals, dragons and satyrs, spells to seduce, spells to harm and many others lay before him.

Then, at last, he found the page he desired. Reading intently, he nodded to himself.

"Yes, Yes ! " he smiled cruelly. "This will do well. And now I need blood of my blood, bone of my bone. He is here. He is close. And I will have him !"

CHAPTER SEVENTEEN

Barnaby gazed around the room and sighed. It was so peaceful here, even though the house was off a busy road near the university. It was a relief to escape from the claustrophobic atmosphere at home where the presence of Le Prevost lingered like a dark cloud, affecting even his father. Barnaby had never seen him so angry. He had insisted that Barnaby was to blame for the loss of the grimoire, despite his protestations of innocence.

When Helen, sensing all was not well in his house, had invited him to stay for a few days, Barnaby's mother had agreed immediately. She needed to regain her full strength and the tension between her husband and Barnaby was too much to bear. Barnaby had been gently teased by his fellow choristers about his new "girlfriend" but he had shrugged it off. He didn't have time for that.

The small box room lay at the back of the house overlooking a lush, tree -lined garden. Barnaby had forgotten how quickly autumn had progressed. The vivid golds and reds had already begun to fade. Perhaps the torrential rainstorms had been responsible, he thought. When he lay on the small but comfortable bed and gazed up at the ceiling, he could see Helen's handiwork, for the surface of the ceiling itself had been painted in an abstract manner to resemble a woodland glade. When he looked closely he had a sense of the shifting of leaves and half concealed forms.

His reverie was broken by Helen's voice.

"Barnaby ! Come down and have some tea !"

The Dark Entry

*   *   *

Barnaby finished the last slice of Mrs Murray's delicious carrot cake and sat back in his chair.

"Oh ! That was wonderful Mrs Murray. Thanks !"

"Barnaby, for goodness' sake, don't be so formal. After all we've been through, please just call me Anne."

Barnaby blushed and smiled.

"Okay, thanks Anne," he said shyly.

"You're welcome here, Barnaby," said Helen. "After all that has happened to you at the cathedral, what with the security officer and the verger, you need a rest. You won't be able to practice in the cathedral anyway, for a while, at least. We need to get together with the others and decide what we're going to do next. Obviously we need to get the grimoire back. Your father, Barnaby, would never believe it if we told him the truth. Isn't that right mum ?"

Anne Murray looked at them both.

"It's up to you four now," she replied. "You all have your individual strengths, even if you don't know it yet. I think that in the end it will be down to you four to fight this fight. No, don't look so alarmed Barnaby, you don't know how strong you really are."

"I'm sorry I haven't been able to find out about the other things in the coffin," said Barnaby. "With the mood he's in at the moment, I just daren't mention them to my father. He'd go berserk ! But look, what worries me is this. I'm a distant relative of this man. I think he's after me for a reason. Problem is I don't know what that is."

"But you are YOU – not him ! Always remember that, Barnaby. You are your own person."

The Dark Entry

That same evening, the object of Barnaby's concern was standing on the top of a small hill near the river. Le Prevost stood straight and tall, his gaunt face etched against the late evening sunlight. It had taken him some time to find this old place again. He simply hadn't recognised it. It had been destroyed. The old chapel lay in ruins. Who on earth could have committed such sacrilege ?

He watched until the last ray of light disappeared in the west, then turned and walked the boundary of his circle, muttering under his breath. Then he returned to the centre of the circle and stood still as a rock, focussing his thoughts. Raising his arms to the darkening sky, he began to utter the words of power. Words dredged up from a long distant past, dragged from the depths of his dark soul. And so the ancient spell took shape and whirled like a mist around him. Birds fell silent in the trees and all sounds of traffic and human life ceased. He stood in the still, quiet centre and beyond the edge of the circle, the winds began to blow and shift, quietly, gathering momentum, then breaking like a wave against the hill and moving outwards over the city.

Still he stood, his power rising ever more, the dark words shooting upwards like small daggers of fire. And still he chanted until the flashes of fire united and danced and became one great forked arrow of flame which shot high into the heavens, illuminating the city from east to west. And the skies darkened to the colour of ebony as the winds became a hurricane.

Then came the thunder, roaring and exploding around the hill, merging and dancing with the lightning.

And so the great storm smashed against the city, uprooting trees, tossing roof tiles in all directions, overturning cars and bicycles as if they were mere toys, cast this way and that by some dark hand. Huge bolts of lightning found their targets. Chimneys, trees, buildings, even people were struck by the terrible flashes of fire that streamed down from the sky. The

The Dark Entry

thunder roared like a vast cannon, ricocheting over rooftops while people cowered below, speechless with fear.

Beyond the city people gathered together to watch the spectacle. The savagery of the storm filled them with trepidation. They had never seen anything like its force or intensity. As each flash of lightning struck its target, they cried out in amazement, and when the winds shifted and turned their way they fled to the fragile safety of their homes.

The storm rolled across the city and thundered about their ears. They trembled, wondering what damage it would cause. This was the time of the equinoctial gales but this hurricane-like wind was bigger and more devastating than anything they had ever experienced. Was this the effect of global warming? So soon?

CHAPTER EIGHTEEN

"I've got to get it back !" said Barnaby. "I've got to make it right with my father or he'll never forgive me !"

He stood with Helen, shivering with apprehension as the storm raged about them. They had huddled in a bus shelter opposite the cathedral for more than twenty minutes, hoping to catch sight of the verger, but he had not yet appeared.

"We'll do our best," said Helen. She shrank back against the side of the shelter as the thunder exploded about them. "Darren and Luke will let us know as soon as they see him." She had to shout against the overpowering noise from above.

Barnaby nodded in reply. There were few people in the streets of the city, all traffic had ceased, and there was a palpable taste of fear in the air. Helen was not surprised that the streets were empty. It had taken some courage for them all to have braved the storm. She felt both fear and exhilaration at each lightning flash and fingered the amulet about her neck. Fire to fire, she thought. She trusted her mother's ability to protect her with this rune, but the sheer electrical force of the storm had unnerved her. She looked up and there, hooded and bent against the wind, appeared Luke. He shouted above the storm: "He's back ! Darren's still there. Stay here for a bit. I'll be in touch." And with that he was gone.

"I don't know how much longer I can stand this," said Barnaby, nervously. "It seems to be getting worse."

"Hold on," said Helen, giving him a hug. "Just a bit longer."

They waited as the pyrotechnic display lit up the sky. It's like a vast firework display which has gone crazy, thought Barnaby. I've never seen anything like it.

The Dark Entry

They didn't have to wait long before Helen's mobile rang. It was Luke.

"Luke! What's up ?"

"He's leaving. Now. We think he's got the book. Come quickly."

The line crackled then broke as the storm disrupted the signal.

"Come on, Barnaby!" said Helen, and they were off down the street.

As they approached Darren and Luke, Barnaby noticed the cloaked figure across the road. His cowled head was bent against the wind and so he did not see them. Barnaby hauled Helen into a shop doorway.

"Quick ! He's there !"

Even now his voice shook as he saw the figure he so dreaded. They waited until he had passed them, with Darren and Luke hot on his heels. The four came together and followed the figure as he approached the cathedral gate.

"Look!" said Darren. "He's got a key. We need to get in quickly."

They watched as he passed into the grounds, hoping desperately he would not lock the gate after him. There was a terrible urgency about his actions as he strode through the opening and down towards the cathedral. He did not seem to notice anything around him, hunched, determined, as if some great, absorbing challenge lay ahead of him.

"Thank God for that!" hissed Luke. "Oops ! Pardon me for that!"

Darren laughed. "Don't take His name in vain, Luke!"

They all smiled, glad of a moment of sanity in this maelstrom of madness. They followed as quietly as they could, the storm raging above them.

Le Prevost approached the Dark Entry. There was no one around and the place was in darkness as he entered. He closed the door quietly behind him.

"Wait !" whispered Darren. They stood, hearts beating, panic rising.

"I've brought what I can," whispered Helen. "I've got my bull roarer and my mother's dark mirror. It's small but it may be useful."

"Good !" said Luke. "Now let's go in. I didn't see him lock the door."

The Dark Entry

Darren quietly opened the great oak door. They cringed as it creaked, then paused before entering.

"Okay," said Luke. "Come on."

There were no lights in the cathedral and the cloisters were cloaked in shadow.

"I think the electricity's been affected by the storm," said Barnaby as they edged their way down the cloister in the direction of the nave. The only light came as brief flashes of lightning shot through the dark passageway, casting strange, flickering shadows on the walls as it did so.

They looked up at the roof bosses and it seemed to them that the shapes and figures had come alive. They moved closer together, uneasy at what they saw. Helen stopped.

"I have to go into the labyrinth," she insisted quietly. "I just have to."

"Not now," groaned Darren. "There isn't time !"

"I have to," she said firmly. "You three go into the nave. See what he's doing in there but be careful. I won't be long, I promise you." With that, she disappeared.

Darren, Luke and Barnaby continued as Helen made her way alone out of the cloister. She stood at the entrance to the labyrinth and took a deep breath. When she was ready, she began her walk, hardly able to see in places but occasionally aided by the lightning. She had trodden this path before many times and was familiar with every twist and turn. She controlled the rising fear of the lightning storm and concentrated solely on the ritual. When she reached the centre of the labyrinth she stopped abruptly and raised her head. With eyes closed, she took off her amulet and held it high in the gloom. Then she opened her eyes and concentrated hard on the runes inscribed on the stone. She knew them off by heart and could see the shape of Fehu, the fire rune, grounded by the earth rune, Elhaz.

She visualized the figure of a tall woman with flaming red hair, robed in a golden cloak, a large amber necklace around her neck. Its stones gleamed like pockets of fire. As her vision deepened, so the fire grew and the face of the woman glowed with light. The trance intensified and the figure became a ball of fire, glowing more and more fiercely until the amulet appeared to throb with a strange heat of its own, sending shafts of warmth through her body. As she looked up to the sky it seemed to her as if the lightning and the amulet had become as one. *I will use his lightning magic against him.* Then, after what seemed an eternity, weariness flooded through her and she sank to her knees.

*   *   *

The others slipped silently into the main body of the cathedral. The darkness felt suffocating and oppressive as they struggled to see where Le Prevost had gone. Then, down towards the altar, they suddenly saw a light. Le Prevost had lit two tall black candles at the high altar. They crept down towards the very place where Barnaby spent so much of his time, the choir stalls. They could see the outline of Le Prevost as he lit yet more candles. Then he stood in the centre of the circle of lights and opened the ancient grimoire.

Barnaby suppressed a cry as he recognised the ornate book. Darren placed a hand firmly over his mouth and frowned a warning. They waited with growing apprehension as the tall, cloaked figure began to chant in Latin. Barnaby's flesh crawled at the sound of the words that seemed so strangely familiar to him. He was half fascinated by what he saw and heard as if it were some distant memory that had come back to haunt him. He feared his connection to this man, this gaunt creature of the dark. What if he should become like him ? What if the seed of his darkness was waiting to grow ?

They continued to watch as, slowly, a vague mist began to form above Le Prevost's head. As the chant gathered pace, so the mist deepened into a

The Dark Entry

dense, dark cloud. Barnaby shook as he realised the meaning of that cloud. Le Prevost was creating some dark, malignant presence, he was sure of it.

So it continued until the mist formed into a crouched shape. Barnaby knew he must do something, anything, to halt this desecration within the cathedral. He could contain himself no longer.

"No !" he shouted. "Stop this ! Not here ! Not in the cathedral !"

There was a stunned silence. He could hardly believe what he had done. Darren and Luke gazed at him in disbelief.

Le Prevost's voice thundered down at them.
"Who is there ?"

The words dissolved into a bestial roar of rage and frustration. They watched in horror as the cloud swirled tightly around Le Prevost's head, then dissipated into nothingness. And then the magician was upon them like a wounded tiger, snarling and growling at them. He stopped abruptly and glared at them, his eyes baleful pinpoints of fire.
"So you think you would stop me ? Children ! Callow youths ! And YOU ! You of my flesh ! Come to me ! NOW !"

Barnaby fought, stepping back from the dark presence. He must not give in. But the command came once more, echoing the thunder from without.

"NOW !"

It was then he stepped slowly forwards, unable to resist.

"At last ! We have work to do ! And you two ! Where is the girl ?"
There was silence.
"Well. You think to harm me ? You think you have the strength to defy me ? Then – deal with this !"

The Dark Entry

Le Prevost seized Barnaby and held him close, then raised his right arm and pointed to the choir stalls. There was a creaking sound like the splitting of wood. The boys turned and stared at the stalls. The familiar places set aside for songs of praise began to shift and alter, the cracking sound growing louder and more insistent until it seemed to fill the cathedral.

They gazed in abject horror as the misericords, so carefully carved, began to move and stretch their dark oak bodies. Darren and Luke moved away, panic rising, unable to comprehend the scene before them.

Down from the tops of the choir stalls came the creatures. Small at first they were, then growing rapidly to their full size. Some snarling, others growling as if to mimic Le Prevost's anger. Here was a wodewose, a wild man of the forest, stinking of damp earth. A lion came with him, struggling on a long leash. There slithered a dark serpent, coiling and uncoiling as if in a dance. Next came a bear, shuffling, arms outstretched, jaws and yellow teeth snapping. And last of all a creature of legend that flew down into the space behind Le Prevost. It was a dragon, its eyes blazing and nostrils filled with acrid smoke.

They turned as one to Le Prevost and greeted him. He smiled cruelly, then, pulling Barnaby with him, left with these words:

"Go to them, my beauties. Do your worst !"

Then Barnaby and Le Prevost were gone.

The Dark Entry

CHAPTER NINETEEN

Barnaby's cries faded into silence, a silence broken only by the sounds of Darren and Luke's heavy breathing. And in the centre of the labyrinth Helen stirred from her dream, aware of a discordant energy that whirled and twisted and roared through the very heart of the cathedral. Alarmed, she leapt to her feet, still weakened from her ritual, then retraced her steps back through the labyrinth and into the cloister. Slipping through the door, she made her way up the nave towards the choir stalls.

There, before her, stood Luke and Darren, frozen with fear, as around them paced a menacing array of creatures. She could hardly believe her eyes. An enormous black bear snarled and pawed the ground as it shifted and lumbered its way closer to Darren. It smelt of decay and corruption and its aged, yellowed teeth gnashed and snapped. A serpent slithered silently towards the two boys, its black tongue darting, eyes cruel and cold. The images in front of her, the wodewose, and dragon, swirled before her eyes. It was as if she had entered into a nightmare.

Then the noise began, such a growling, roaring and bellowing as had never before been heard in this holy place. The silence broken, Darren and Luke turned and fled towards the door, the bear close behind them. Seeing the stunned Helen standing rooted to the spot, they grabbed her and pushed her out into the darkened cloister. There they paused, breathing hard, fear coursing through them.

But they had no time to rest. The menagerie burst through the door, bringing with it such a primeval force that the young people were stunned by the impact. The dragon was the only creature that was unable to advance, its body wedged in the doorway, its wings just too large to clear the space. It struggled to push through, inching slowly forwards, flapping

The Dark Entry

its wings, head twisting with frustration. Roaring its anger at them, it opened its wide jaws and a stream of rank, sulphurous fire burst from its black nostrils.

"We've got to do something !" shouted Darren above the tumult. "We've got to stop them getting out of the cathedral. Come on ! Pull yourselves together. Amulets !"

At these words, the other two shook themselves. It seemed to them that Darren had grown in stature as he drew up the energy from the earth, his sign, his element.

Darren, Luke and Helen stood in a line halfway down the cloister, facing the oncoming threat. Then, to their horror, Darren strode forward to meet the bear. The bear reared high and roared its challenge, clawing the air. Darren's own animal instinct surged up in response and his own answering bellow echoed through the cloister. Helen was amazed at the power of his voice.

The bear swiped at Darren, his great paw knocking him to the ground. Helen cried out as Darren staggered to his feet, his shoulder streaming with blood.
"Amulet !" she cried. "Use it ! NOW !"

Through a mist of pain, he heard her words and his hand fumbled for the stone. As his fingers touched it a warmth spread through his body and into his shoulder. Gathering his strength, Darren raised the stone high, the runic shape facing the bear. And then the stone began to hum, gathering pace, a deep, low sound born of the earth, a sound as hard as granite, and as pure as crystal. It pierced the stones of the cathedral. Helen and Luke staggered back, holding their heads in pain, trying to shut out the deep rumbling sound. They clasped their amulets for protection and their pain eased.

The bear began to retreat, its massive head twisting this way and that in a desperate attempt to rid itself of the overwhelming noise. The stone's deep sound reached a pitch of such intensity that the great creature

The Dark Entry

staggered and fell, writhing on the flagstones and the sound of the earth penetrated deep into its body. It creaked and split and from its heart there rose a smell of old decaying wood.

Above them the lightning still blazed, illuminating the scene. It was then they saw that the bear had returned to its original form. No more than an oak carving, riven and shattered into pieces.

Nothing now moved in the silence of the cloister. Beasts and humans were stunned by the sequence of events. The carved creatures had cowered back, retreating from the overwhelming noise but now they recovered their senses and moved forwards, sensing their prey.

The wodewose and the lion closed steadily on Darren, the great beast roaring its challenge. Luke instinctively moved to Darren's side, aware of his bleeding wound and fading strength.

The wild man of the woods threw down his leash, which had contained the lion for so long and, like the hunter that he was, moved in for the kill. The crouched figure, leaf-clad and reeking of damp earth, leaves and rotting bark, moved like a panther, closer and closer. Its claw-nailed hands stretched out towards him. Darren, taking a deep breath, faced him.

Luke moved to face the lion. He could communicate with many creatures, but his fear of this savage beast almost overcame him. He stilled his mind and projected thoughts of calm and peace towards the great head.

The lion paused and stared back at him, as if suddenly confused. Luke clutched his amulet and felt the comforting surge of power he had felt by the river. The lion reacted and sat back on its haunches. Luke focussed his thoughts into a shape of light and sent it gently into the mind of the beast.

His first impression was of a wall of chaos, seething with images of hunger, anger and the desire to kill. The force of the savagery astounded him and he stepped back, away from the lion, away from this force. The amulet slipped from his fingers and hung from his neck like a discarded stone. The lion reared up, roaring once more. Luke's blood ran cold.

114

The Dark Entry

It was almost upon him before he had the wit to grasp his amulet once more with an intensity of concentration that surprised him. He channelled the power from the stone and flung it hard at the lion. The creature whimpered and staggered back. Luke advanced and, seizing the leash, forced the lion towards the side of the cloister. The effort almost overwhelmed him and he felt his strength begin to drain from his body. As he weakened, so the lion roused itself once more. All Luke could see in the mind of the beast were images of blood and raw flesh and an intense hunger. With one last effort he dragged the chain around a stone pillar and secured it as well as he could, then retreated, stumbling backwards as he went.

Just a short distance down the cloister Darren wrestled with the wodewose. It was all he could do to keep the clawed hands contained. The wild man snarled and hissed at him as Darren held him in a bear hug. *He's so strong and I have little strength left.* Small, beady eyes glared at him from a bush of matted hair and he bared his fang-like teeth, snapping at Darren's neck. The breath was rank and foul. Then the teeth found their mark as the wodewose bit at his wounded shoulder.

Darren bellowed in pain. Anger surged through him. He seized the hair of the man-beast and yanked it sharply back until the creature released his jaws. Darren held him fast, then twisted him round and pushed him up hard against the stone wall.

Helen stood her ground near the Dark Entry as the serpent slid towards her. It reared up in front of her, its great hooded head level with her own. It swayed from side to side, its slatted eyes holding her gaze, unblinking. She felt powerless to move as the hypnotic power of the snake began to sap her will. The black tongue flicked and darted as if in anticipation. *I must move or I'm in big trouble.*

Her hand slid into her pocket. To the penny whistle she had hastily tucked in there before she left home. As if in a dream, still enchanted, she lifted the whistle to her lips and began to play. The notes rose, slow and repetitive like an ancient mantra, filling the cloisters with a haunting sound. And gradually the serpent succumbed to the rhythm of the whistle, its head slowly sinking down, as if bowing to her. Still she played, caught up in the magic of the music. And still the serpent sank lower and coiled in on itself. She did not dare stop the flow and continued as the serpent closed its eyes.

And so the bizarre scene unfolded: Darren holding fast the wodewose, but strength draining; Luke, leaning exhausted against the cloister wall, face pale; the lion straining against its leash; Helen playing her magic to the serpent. And then the sound of splintering wood shook the air.

With a final heave, the dragon thrust its way through the door, scraping its wings against the jamb, roaring in triumph and rage, a stream of fire blazing forth.

"Darren ! Luke ! Come here ! Remember, they're just wood !"

Helen's voice seemed small and weak but they heard her. Darren smashed the wodewose's head hard against the stone pillar, then ran to join Luke. The two sprinted down the length of the cloister as the dragon began to move, unable to use its wings in the confines of the place. The wodewose, concussed, stumbled into its path in blind panic and was promptly incinerated. The lion roared its defiance, straining against its chain, enraged at this new threat. With one last twist of its head, it broke the chain and sprang at the dragon's head, growling and snapping sharp teeth. The dragon's jaws opened wide once more and the lion was engulfed in flame.

The serpent had been roused from its trance when the music had stopped and now raised its head, looking for its prey. Sensing the movement ahead, it slithered over the cobbles, rearing up as it went. As the dragon drew close, it lunged towards it, fangs glistening with venom, but the great winged creature proved too great a foe and, seizing its head in its massive jaws, with one vicious bite, broke the serpent's neck. As the snake expired, its flesh turned back to wood and the dragon spat it out, recoiling.

The Dark Entry

"It's coming for us next !" shouted Luke. "I can't cope with that. The lion was enough for me ! Into the Dark Entry. Come on !"

"We've had it !" groaned Darren in despair.
The three slipped through the doorway into the Dark Entry.
"At least it can't get us in here," said Helen.
"No, but the fire can !" said Darren.

The dragon stopped at the doorway, its dark eye peering through, sniffing the air.
"It's short sighted," whispered Helen.
It lowered its long neck at the sound of her voice.
"Do something, Helen !" said Luke. "It'll be like an oven in here. Le Prevost has locked the door. We're trapped !"

The dragon drew back its great head as if preparing its fire. Helen clasped her amulet and thought of Freya, the golden one, and of her amber, gold of the North. She felt its warmth spread within her and the warmth became a fire and from the amulet there now burst a ray of white heat. As the dragon prepared to strike, so the white heat grew stronger and enveloped the roaring creature. Fire met with fire and with one great explosion the dragon disappeared.

CHAPTER TWENTY

Down the cloister strode Le Prevost, dragging the struggling, fearful boy behind him.

"You will not see your friends again !" sneered Le Prevost. "The creatures will take care of them !"
Barnaby turned cold with fear.

Through the Dark Entry they passed. Le Prevost pulled the door open wide, locked it, then paused for a moment outside. It was dark and overhead the storm still raged, illuminating the dark sky. Then he threw back his head and howled into the wind like some feral beast.

"And this is what you have done to my world ! Boxes for houses, flimsily made, great buildings maimed and destroyed, armies of monstrous wagons rampaging through the streets, reeking of poison ! Is this my inheritance ?"

Barnaby struggled to free himself but his captor's iron grip held him fast. They pressed onwards, across the Lower Close and down Pull's Ferry Lane.
"And here, here was a canal. Where is it ? Covered and hidden."

So they continued, Barnaby struggling to keep up and Le Prevost ranting and cursing the world he had found. The gates along the river proved no barrier to him, though they had been locked at sunset. Across Bishop's Bridge they went and past a large pub, almost empty now because of the raging storm. No one saw them, the tall, lean, black-clad man and the young choirboy, held tight in his grasp, shivering with fear as the storm raged round them, all thunder and lightning but no rain. It was as if they

The Dark Entry

were invisible to others, bound within their own world. A man, making his way across the bridge, did not even see them. Barnaby was in despair. No one could help him now. His friends must have deserted him.

On they travelled, up a steep hill to Kett's Heights, a steep, partially wooded enclosure, hidden behind a wall. They made their way up the path, occasionally losing their footing in the dark. Only the flashes of lightning aided their journey. Halfway up, Le Prevost paused for breath. Panting heavily, he turned to Barnaby.

"All this was wooded once," he cried above the thunder. "And now all these roads and dwellings choke its spirit."

"But none of it is my fault !" said Barnaby, weakly. He found speech difficult as if some force clutched at his throat. "Let me go !"

Le Prevost, ignoring his plea, strode onwards, the path winding ahead among trees and overgrown thickets, sometimes rising up before them, then dropping away at their feet. He was relentless, contemptuous of his hostage's weakened state, and when Barnaby finally could walk no further, he lifted him and carried him up to the top, slung over his shoulder like a sack, as if he were as light as a feather. His strength had grown steadily, feeding on some inner, urgent need to fulfil his task.

At last they came to a wide clearing, surrounded by trees. To one side stood the ivy covered walls of an ancient ruined chapel. Le Prevost lowered Barnaby down onto the earth in the centre of the grassy area, and then strode vigorously around the glade.

"Here once stood the chapel of St Michael, where prayers were said for the dead. See what has become of it !"

Barnaby struggled weakly.

"You WILL listen to me, boy! You WILL understand what your people have done to my world!"

He stepped back, face dark with anger, then turned and disappeared into the trees. Barnaby slowly sat up and looked round. Where was he? Could he escape ? He called out, his throat easing a little. There was no

119

reply save the sound of the storm. He called again, stretching his body as he stood.

"Do not move !" Le Prevost's sharp voice commanded as he appeared in a gap between two oak trees. "No one can hear you, boy! No one will come to your aid! I have such powers that you would only dream of! Stay still!"

With that command his voice altered and deepened and he began to utter archaic words. Barnaby's body stiffened. He tried to move his legs but it was impossible. They were locked tight as if in a vice, as if by magic. Le Prevost approached with a bundle of torches.

"I have it all ready," he said, smiling coldly. "I have been preparing for this moment."

He placed the torches at regular intervals in a large circle around Barnaby. Then, snapping his fingers, each one flamed high, illuminating the scene with eerie, dancing shadows. Le Prevost's gaunt face gazed down at Barnaby like some giant bird of prey, head cocked to one side, eyes penetrating and black.

"Now my boy, you will learn your fate!"

Reaching into his pocket, he took out a length of thin, strong rope and bound Barnaby's hands and feet. Then he lifted him and laid him almost tenderly on the ground. He peered at Barnaby's amulet and for a moment recoiled sharply. He tried to touch it but as soon as his hand neared it he felt a sharp pain shoot through his hand and up his arm.

"Aaah!" He clutched his throbbing fingers and cursed, then, finding a stick on the ground nearby, he gingerly lifted the cord of the amulet from around Barnaby's neck, pulling his head up to do so. He hurled the amulet like a catapult towards the trees. Bereft of the stone, Barnaby felt lost and totally alone. The amulet had kept him going throughout this nightmare and now he felt his energy drain from him. Then Le Prevost knelt beside him and spoke.

"You must know, my boy, that you are of my blood. Through the centuries we are linked, more closely than you might know. The woman

The Dark Entry

who betrayed me bore my child, without my knowledge, and so the line continued through each generation. She brought about my end. I curse her for that. So badly treated was I – I who was the prior, a man of importance, yet even so I died at the hands of the mob."

He paused, eyes burning with old memories.

"And so I was deprived of all my magical apparatus. But you, you have given me the one thing I needed. My grimoire. The other objects I regret I do not have save the ring, but this book and this ring, these treasures are my gateway back into the past."

Taking the book from beneath his cloak, he fingered the cover with quiet reverence.

"I must return to the time before the betrayal and reclaim that which was lost. And then I will wreak such havoc and vengeance that the world will tremble in my presence !"

He paused again, then that cruel smile appeared.

"And your world, dear Barnaby, dear blood of my blood, your tawdry woeful world that lacks so much magic and has such contempt for the natural order, will simply cease to be. It will be expunged utterly. The pathway of the present will be peeled back and a new order will arise. When I have taken my revenge the new world will emerge in my image."

He stood and stretched his limbs, pacing around Barnaby's inert body, laughing and mumbling to himself. Barnaby's thoughts struggled to make sense of what he had heard. A feeling of desperation gripped him. There was nothing he could do to stop Le Prevost. His friends must have been destroyed by now and surely those creatures would be loose upon the city.

Now he was truly alone. No one could help him. He was at the mercy of this madman from the past. He had no idea what Le Prevost would do with him, but he feared the worst. If he was of the same bloodline, was he also capable of such darkness? Had he brought this misfortune upon his friends? He watched the man in spite of himself. Should he play for time, waiting for his chance to escape? It was worth a shot.

The Dark Entry

"We're related. Look, we could work together. I could help you. There must be some of you in my genes."

He hated himself for saying these things but he had no choice. His voice was weak.

Le Prevost turned to Barnaby. There was a nervous energy about him as he gazed down at the young boy. It was as if Barnaby had not spoken. The man was deep into his madness, fixed into his thoughts and wild imaginings.

"You know how the human spirit can travel through time?" began Le Prevost. "In my rituals I had been able to move through time, only a short distance, but corporeally…"

"What is that?" asked Barnaby, his voice weaker now.

"It means that both spirit and body could breach time's barrier. I did this first with a mouse, then I progressed to a dog. Oh, such a necromancer was I !"

His voice swelled with pride as he continued.

"Then there was a small infant I took from a beggar woman. I transported her too. All these beings I moved to other locations. It was a success! Then I continued my studies but the mob interrupted the final stages of my greatest work!"

He stopped and looked at Barnaby thoughtfully.

"But now I have *you*. You are my link between past and present. You will be my channel back to my time where I belong. You are like me. I see the darkness, my darkness, inside you. There it lies, hidden like a jewel, waiting to be brought out into the light. My legacy has lived on in you, my boy. And I shall use it, very soon."

He looked at Barnaby almost affectionately and stooped to stroke his hair.

The Dark Entry

"You, Barnaby, will be my sacrifice!"

The Dark Entry

CHAPTER TWENTY ONE

The three stood in the narrow space and watched as the dragon burned, the wood cracking and smoking.

"How are we going to get out?" demanded Luke.
"I don't have enough strength yet," said Helen, her face pale and blackened with smoke.
"We'll have to force it," said Darren, reaching into his pocket and producing a screwdriver. "I've kept this with me, specially with all these violent people around at the moment."

The other two looked on as he attacked the lock.
"We'll lose Barnaby," said Helen, frantically. "He'll be long gone. Hurry up, Darren!"
"I'm trying," shouted Darren irritably. "This is a tough one!"

It took fifteen minutes, then there was a sharp crack as the lock broke.

"At last!" cried Luke as they staggered through the Dark Entry, coughing and spluttering from the sulphurous smoke.

"That was so close!" croaked Luke, throat dry and parched.

They stumbled on through the Lower Close in a desperate effort to distance themselves from all that happened. Helen collapsed onto a wooden bench, trying to regain her breath, and the others soon joined her.

"It's gone! The storm has passed! All of a sudden…" gasped Helen.
"And Le Prevost and Barnaby have gone, too!" said Darren. "We have to find them!"
"They could be anywhere – miles away by now!" exclaimed Luke.

The Dark Entry

"I'm not so sure of that," said Helen. "I'm sure he needs Barnaby for something but I don't know what. But I'm so afraid for him."

"Well – where might he be?" asked Darren. "We need to get on. There may not be much time left."

"I don't think he will have gone into the city," said Luke thoughtfully. "I think we should go this way. I think he'd need somewhere quiet and private, don't you? "

And with that he headed off down Ferry Lane towards the river. The others followed, quiet and pensive, unsure about their direction. What if Luke was wrong? When they reached the water's edge, they stopped, uncertain whether to turn left or right.

It was then the owl appeared, swooping silently down, almost colliding with Luke. Its green eyes stared at them.

"It's the barn owl!" shouted Luke. "It helped me. Do you remember when I saw the creatures in the river?"

"Yes, " replied Helen. "Why has it come back to you?"

Luke stared up at the owl's white, heart shaped face. Its luminous eyes gazed back at him, unblinking as it perched on a tree. Then it lifted slowly up from the branch, flapped its wings and flew in the direction of Bishop's Bridge. It paused on the back of a seat and waited.

"I think it's wanting us to follow," said Helen. Luke closed his eyes and concentrated hard. He entered the strange, alien mind of the owl. It was like swimming in fog. Odd, distorted images drifted in and out but at the centre he clearly saw Barnaby's face. There was an urgency about its thoughts and it flew further along the path before pausing again.

"Come on!" said Darren. "We can't hang about! Let's go."

The three made their way to the bridge. It was dark now and if it had not been for the owl's white presence ahead of them, they might well have lost their way.

"Hold on," said Luke, and he rummaged through his pocket. "Ah! Gotcha!" he said triumphantly. "My magna torch. I use it for fishing. Come on then."

125

The Dark Entry

Across the bridge they ran, the owl and the small beam of light guiding their way.

"I know where we're going," said Luke, pausing for breath, lungs still bruised with smoke.

"Where?" panted Darren.

"Kett's Heights. The old hill. That's where."

And so they found their way to the hill above the city. Through the iron gates a narrow curving path beckoned.

"This is it!" called Luke. "This is Kett's Heights." Helen and Darren followed him as he made his way up the slope.

"I can't see anything," said Helen, her voice rising with trepidation. But they continued up the winding pathway. Halfway up the steep slope they were brought up short by the sight of a wall of strange shapes and as they drew closer, they were horrified to see an army of troll-like creatures, tall and strong and fierce.

Luke groaned. "This is his doing. He must be here somewhere."

Darren picked up a stout branch lying across the path.

"Arm yourselves," he shouted, then turned to face the threat. "As if we haven't had enough already!"

So there they stood, the three companions, grim faced and resolute. And ahead of them a great barrier of grotesque, misshapen figures crouched, waiting for combat.

"Wait," whispered Luke. "Something's not right."

"What?" asked Helen.

"They're not what they seem."

He stood, eyes closed, as his mind attempted to link and meld with the creatures ahead of him. Then, astonishingly, he laughed. The other two gazed at him in amazement.

The Dark Entry

"They're not trolls," he said. "It's the rats again. Shapeshifting!"

"Right," said Darren, firmly, and he strode ahead, his branch flashing and flailing as he laid into the crowd. "Leave this lot to me. You go on," he shouted as he waded into the throng. All trace of the trolls disappeared as he advanced, leaving only a pack of chittering rats, scurrying and darting in an effort to block his path.

Helen and Luke cleared a gap with their sticks, battering at the gnashing rodents, sending them flying through the air.

"Come on, Helen!" said Luke, seizing her by the hand. "We must find Barnaby."

And so they ran on up the pathway whilst Darren continued his attack. His hands and legs were bleeding from the bites and scratches of the rats but he took no notice, hardly feeling the pain.

Helen and Luke reached the clearing. There they saw the circle of glittering torches. In the centre lay Barnaby, bound hand and foot with Le Prevost standing over him.

"Oh no!" whispered Helen. "We may be too late."

"What's he doing ?" asked Luke.

"A ritual – but I don't know what sort of ritual."

Le Prevost stood back from Barnaby and, holding out his grimoire, his ringed hand glinting in the torchlight, began slowly to chant. The language was strangely archaic and made no sense to the two watchers. Then he walked the boundary of the circle, his forefinger pointing rigidly, sealing its circumference. He strode to the centre of the circle where Barnaby lay helpless, raised his arms high and began his invocation. The voice was harsh but stronger now, the tone demanding as if conjuring the spirits.

At the edge of the clearing Helen and Luke shivered. There was nothing they could do to help their friend.

The Dark Entry

"I think he's calling up something terrible," said Helen, "some demon from the dark. He's using the ring to summon it. I wish my mother were here. She'd know what to do."

The voice intensified, cruel and soulless, and from the ring a harsh red light blazed high above Le Prevost. From its centre a creature slowly took shape. A winged being with a human head and leathery skin, and at the tip of its long tail was a lethal barb. Hands with razor sharp talons clawed the air and the face was the stuff of nightmares. A sharp, narrow face, with deep set, slanted red eyes peered down at Le Prevost. Brilliant white fangs were bared in a grimace and the bat-like wings beat in a harsh rhythm as the creature landed on the earth. It paced and hissed as it circled the magician, then threw back its head and screamed.

The sound rose, tearing the air into shreds. It was a shrill, ear piercing sound like a drill penetrating bone. Then Le Prevost snapped his fingers. The creature hissed once more, then became still.

Helen's voice was small and troubled.
"I know what that thing is. It's a harpy. I've seen such things in old books. It's a creature from the shadowlands."
Luke was silent. There would be no communicating with *this* creature.

As they continued to watch, a small white bird landed to their right.
"It's the owl!" exclaimed Luke, "It's still here!"
The owl turned and offered them its unblinking gaze once more, then stooped and gathered up an object which lay at its feet. Then it flew up into the air and around the circle.
"That's Barnaby's amulet." whispered Helen. "I'm sure of it!" She could see the outline of it in the torchlight,

Three times round the perimeter it flew, then drifted into the circle itself.
"How did it do that?" gasped Luke. "What sort of an owl is that?"
"It's a long story, but it's a creature from the underworld. A messenger. Even so, I don't know where it's come from, or what power it has."

The Dark Entry

They saw the owl bravely fly across to where Barnaby lay. Then it swooped low, dropping the amulet on his chest. It was a brave undertaking for the bird, risking all. For not only did it give Barnaby his strength once more through the stone but it also broke the spell of the circle. The combination of the amulet and the power of the owl had been too strong for Le Prevost's magic. The amulet had landed squarely on Barnaby's body and the owl was rising up when the harpy moved. It too was a creature out of time. It was fast and lethal. The owl screeched once, then was silent. Luke jumped to his feet in outrage.

"No!" he shouted, distraught at the sight of the broken white shape, crumpled on the earth.

Le Prevost whirled round, furious at the intrusion.

"Still alive?" he rasped. "Too late! Back into the past. Fly fast, fly fast. Back to the time of my power, heed well the day and the hour!"

The Dark Entry

CHAPTER TWENTY TWO

As he stood over Barnaby, the harpy flew widdershins around the circle. The circle shimmered and shifted as Le Prevost repeated the spell and the harpy flew faster and faster. Neither Le Prevost nor the harpy sensed the broken circle, such was their absorption in the ritual but Helen did notice. Grasping her amulet, she seized Luke's hand and began a summoning of her own.

This was her greatest test. All she had learned from her mother now came to the fore. She invoked a pillar of fire, just as she had done in the cathedral. The resistance from the inside of the circle was enormous. It took every ounce of Helen's strength to maintain her concentration. Luke held her arm as he touched his own amulet. This time there was no water but pure strength that flowed from his body into hers.

So the pillar of fire began to travel round the circle, burning to a white heat. Helen did the best she could, but the circle of fire was patchy and to her horror she saw the harpy screech to a halt and begin to advance. Now it would be free to get out.

Summoning her last drop of energy, she called out, loud and clear: "Barnaby, sing! It is your power. Sing!"

Still the harpy made for her, face twisted with demonic hatred. Barnaby struggled against the force of Le Prevost. He was NOT like him. He must help the others. Barnaby found his strength at last and a clear high voice sounded from the centre of the circle. His strength gave Helen and Luke a few more precious seconds to renew their energy. The harpy stopped dead and listened.

Le Prevost bellowed his rage and summoned the creature.

The Dark Entry

"Back! Back to your work!" he demanded.

The harpy turned and faced Helen and Luke once more. It moved to the edge of the circle and stepped over the line. Helen's fire wavered and fear filled her. It was then she felt a firm, steadying arm around her waist.

"I'm here," said Darren. He was bleeding and ripped but his strength filled her as he clasped his amulet hard.

The harpy stopped and stared at them, then a twisted grin appeared as it moved in for the kill. *My mother's mirror ! It's all I have left.* And she fumbled in her deep pocket. There she felt the sharp, polished stone of the dark mirror. She could almost taste the harpy's breath as she tugged the mirror out of her pocket and raised it before the creature's face.

Through her weariness, words came to her, from where she did not know, but they were both ancient, yet familiar. She thought of her mother. Her voice rose, sharp and clear, and as the harpy gazed down at the mirror, it recoiled. Whatever it saw there in that dark mirror forced it back into the circle, screeching with rage. The last of Helen's strength dropped away and the fire died down. The three stepped forward into the circle. They must rescue Barnaby.

And the harpy turned, thwarted, unable to gain its freedom from servitude, and turned to the one who had imprisoned it. Revenge was its sole emotion now as it seized Le Prevost and enveloped him in its fearsome embrace, its leathery wings and white fangs reaching for him, barbed tail lashing him. He screamed.

"Help me ! Blood of my blood !"

As the harpy's grip tightened, Le Prevost's eyes glazed and, to Helen's astonishment, a dark, thick substance curled and twisted from his gaping mouth. The spirit of Le Prevost was stronger now, dense and substantial through the power he had summoned from the shadow world. She could almost see a glimpse of a narrow, hawk-like face in the miasma as it fled the verger's body in its attempt to save itself. But the harpy was too quick. Releasing the body, it encircled the darkened form with its powerful wings, trapping the two in a tight embrace. Beneath them, the verger's

The Dark Entry

body fell awkwardly to the ground. He stirred, confused and dazed, his head throbbing from the effects of his unwanted visitor. He dragged himself up, then staggered wildly around the circle, unable to comprehend any of the drama that had taken place around him, his brain dulled and half emptied, unable to function any more. Reaching the edge of the trees, he turned once and then fell, tumbling down the bank into the undergrowth. Helen was unable to help him. His blank-eyed face filled her with sorrow.

"Get Barnaby!" shouted Luke to Darren. "Now!"

Darren ran to Barnaby and started to untie the ropes that bound him. Helen and Luke slowly joined him, weariness dragging at them.

Around them the world began to spin. Once started, Le Prevost's spell could not be undone. Helen, Darren and Luke clung to Barnaby as their heads spun and nausea filled them. As the world reeled about them, Le Prevost and the harpy began to slowly fade.

The four friends succumbed, collapsing senseless to the ground.

So the spinning increased and time shifted and swirled around them in a vast maelstrom of sound and images. Then, quite suddenly, they were gone, leaving an empty, torch - lit clearing on Kett's Heights and a bruised and bewildered verger, stumbling his way slowly down the hill.

*   *   *

The four figures lay motionless on the hill. One by one they stirred, then sat up and gazed around them.

132

The Dark Entry

There was no sign of the harpy, Le Prevost or the verger. Indeed there was nothing familiar about Ketts Heights at all, no trees around them, just a bare, grass-covered mound.

Battered and weary, they stood together in a huddle and looked into the distance. There was no city of Norwich, no buildings or roads. Nothing recognisable.

Forest-covered hills and valleys stretched to the horizon.

There was no sign of human life.